D1529013

# THE WAITING ROOM

Copyright © 2025

All rights reserved.

ISBN-13:979-8-28-482216-6

For the memory of my mother, Arlene Carlon,
whose love echoes beyond this world and whose spirit lives
on in every page.

## Author's Note

In the span of thirteen months, I lost both my brother and my mother. Their passings, while profoundly painful, offered unexpected moments of beauty, peace, and connection—particularly in the sacred hours I spent by their bedsides. During that time, I witnessed what many who've experienced end-of-life care will understand: moments that feel like something more than coincidence. Dreams that feel like visits. Conversations that feel like farewells, even before the last breath is taken.

The Waiting Room was my way of processing those experiences. Writing this novel helped me explore the emotional complexity of saying goodbye, the spiritual mystery of what may come next, and the unfinished business so many of us carry into those final chapters with the people we love.

While much of this story is inspired by real events—yes, there were painful phone calls to relatives and even conversations about packed suitcases for "a trip"—this is a work of fiction. The characters, their relationships, and the arcs of their journeys are imagined. They are not stand-ins for me, my family, or anyone I know.

There may be a temptation to see the author in the protagonist's shoes. That's natural. But this is not my story.

Rather, it is a story shaped by personal truths, told through fictional voices. My hope is that readers will find in it a reflection of their own experiences with loss, love, and maybe even a touch of grace.

If this book brings you comfort, opens a door to a difficult conversation, or simply reminds you that you're not alone in your grief, then it has done its job.

With gratitude,
    Michael Carlon

# 1

Mary Mazzone stood impatiently by the elevator just beyond security at Holy Family Hospital in Stamford, Connecticut. Snowflakes clung to her hair, like remnants of a hasty blessing, melting into small streams that traced her face, foreshadowing the tears soon to come. She pressed the "up" button repeatedly, half-wondering if the elevator was hamster-powered, even as she knew her frantic button-mashing wouldn't help. Elevators simply didn't work like that. As the seconds dragged on, the dull hum of hospital chatter and the sterile smell of antiseptic only heightened her frustration.

Mary had sped down the Merritt Parkway from her graduate school in Fairfield, where she was pursuing a Master of Social Work degree at Sacred Heart University. She had been in the middle of a meeting with her advisor when the call came in from her grandfather's oncologist—he was being moved from intensive care, where he had spent the past three days, to Holy Family's palliative care unit. The news hit her like a rush of guilt right before confession—sharp, immediate, and overwhelming—and she was out the door before she could even process it, her mind already racing with what lay ahead.

At long last, the elevator doors opened, and a seemingly impossible number of people exited; doctors, nurses, and visitors all on their way to somewhere more uplifting than a hospice unit. Once the clown car emptied, Mary got in and pushed the button for floor five, where the palliative care unit was housed. As the doors closed, she resisted the urge to jab the button again out of sheer habit.

The ride up was agonizingly slow. With each jarring lurch of the elevator, Mary prayed her grandfather could hold on just a few minutes longer, long enough for her to say goodbye. When the doors finally opened on the fifth floor, she rushed into the hallway, where fluorescent lights buzzed softly, their sterile glow bouncing off pale walls. The faint hum of Silent Night drifted through the air, growing louder with every step she took toward the nurse's station, the bittersweet melody tightening her throat. Once there, Mary found herself face-to-face with Evelyn Thompson, whose poised and calming demeanor stood in stark contrast to her own.

"Now, sugar, there ain't no need to run. This is a hospice floor, not a gymnasium."

Evelyn's flawless mocha-toned skin gleamed under the harsh hospital lights, a subtle reflection of her quiet strength and dedication. Mary guessed she was in her late sixties and was amazed at how she moved so gracefully from her chair at the desk to where Mary was standing.

With a soft drawl that hinted at her Georgia roots, Evelyn's voice carried a warmth that could soothe even the most restless patient. She had the grace of a Southern belle, yet there was a no-nonsense edge to her, honed through years of experience in hospice care. She wore her blue scrubs with the quiet confidence of someone who knew exactly what was needed to bring comfort in the most difficult moments. A faint scent of azalea, the flower that had always reminded

Evelyn of home, hit Mary in the nose.

"I'm sorry… my grandfather… I just…" Mary struggled to get the words out, her chest heaving from the sprint down the hall and the anxiety brewing in her body.

"Take a moment, child," Evelyn said softly, her voice so steady and reassuring, it seemed to help bring Mary's heart rate down. "You must be here for Thomas. He's in room 1012. I'm Evelyn, his nurse, but everyone here calls me Evvie." She placed a gentle hand on Mary's shoulder, offering a small smile. "Let me show you to him."

"I'm Mary, his granddaughter. I got a call that they were moving him from Intensive Care down to here. I was scared I was too late," Mary said, her breathing back under her control.

"Aw, you ain't too late, baby. He told me he's gonna wait for you," Evvie said, walking Mary down the corridor, their footsteps muffled like a sin whispered in a confessional.

"I sped down here from school after getting the call. All I could think of was him dying alone."

"Now listen to me, sugar, this is not the night to be speeding, roads slick with snow and all. You don't want to wind up a guest in our emergency department on Christmas Eve. Gonna be a full house down there I'm afraid. Always is on holidays."

They stopped in front of room 1012. The door was ajar. Mary peeked in at her grandfather, who was sleeping peacefully beneath the dim glow of an overhead lamp.

"Has he been awake at all today?" Mary asked.

"In and out, but now he looks just like a sleeping angel. Go in and be with him, child. I'll be nearby if you need me. We only have one other guest in this unit tonight and there's another nurse working with me so I'm here when you need me."

Mary nodded and walked in the room as Evvie headed

back to the nurse's station, leaving the faint smell of azaleas lingering in the air. After setting her bag on a chair beside her grandfather's bed, she slipped off her coat, draping it over the back of the chair. She then bent over and gave her grandfather a gentle kiss on the forehead. "Geepo, I have no idea if you can hear me, but it's Mary. I'm here."

The nickname had stuck ever since Mary, as a toddler, struggled to pronounce grandpa. Her grandfather, Thomas, had embraced the mispronunciation wholeheartedly, turning it into a term of endearment that felt like a secret word in the unique language they shared. The bond between them had only deepened over the years, as they spent countless hours together.

Thomas never missed a performance, a game, or a milestone in her life. Among his two children, only one had given him a grandchild—and Mary was it. As far as Thomas was concerned, one was all he needed. She had been the light of his life, and the feeling was mutual. They were as thick as thieves, partners in a lifelong adventure of inside jokes, shared stories, and unconditional love.

"I love you, Geepo." Mary looked down at her grandfather's face and saw his lips curl into the faintest of smiles, but he remained silent. She moved to the window, brushing aside the curtain, and saw snow falling heavily outside, the flakes illuminated like tiny stars, as if heaven itself were scattering blessings over the earth.

"I wish you could see this, Geepo. It's gonna be a white Christmas." Mary shook her head. "Who am I kidding, you can't hear me, can you?"

A soft knock at the door stole her attention from the serene scene outside. Mary turned to see Evvie holding a tray.

"The cafeteria is about to close, so I had a tray sent up for you. It might be a long night, baby."

Mary took the tray, her stomach betraying its hunger, a

humble reminder of the fasting she'd do on Ash Wednesday and Good Friday, taking after her grandfather's Catholic traditions. "I'm surprised you didn't hear my stomach growling from the nurses' station."

"Who says I didn't?" Evvie joked. "Anyone else coming tonight? I can probably scrounge up another if I ask soon."

Setting the food down on a tray table, Mary shook her head. "My mom is scrambling to get a flight from Fort Lauderdale, without any luck so far. My Uncle Jack isn't picking up."

"Well, ain't you a peach for being here for him all by yourself."

Mary sat in the chair beside the bed and glanced at her grandfather. "I'd do anything for him. He's been my rock. Taught me how to tie my shoes, ride a bike, and laugh when life got heavy. I just can't believe I'm here, watching him slip away."

Evvie took a few steps closer, once again placing a comforting hand on Mary's shoulder. "It's hard, child. I know. Not just from my work, but from losing all my grandparents, who came to Georgia from Ghana, and my parents. It's never easy, but in time, you might see this as a gift."

"I'd literally ask Santa for anything else this Christmas."

Evvie's gentle smile seemed to warm Mary from the inside out. "I get it, sugar. But there's a reason you're here. A reason he chose you. You may not see it now, but you will in time. Oh, and about that question you asked earlier, about whether he can hear you?"

Mary couldn't believe Evvie had heard her, just minutes before. "You have my mother's hearing."

"It's a quiet night, and I hear everything around here. I do believe our guests in your grandfather's state can hear everything, too, even if they don't respond. So, please keep talking to him."

Mary nodded.

"Oh, and one more thing. Sometimes at this stage our guests may get a sudden burst of energy. They may spring up and talk like their old selves again, maybe even telling you about a dream they had."

Mary's eyes filled with a combination of hope and excitement, like a child hearing the shuffling of footsteps in their home after midnight on Christmas morning. "Does that mean he has more time?"

"I'm afraid not, sugar. The opposite really. But if it does happen, it's a gift, a chance to say what needs saying. Don't waste it."

Mary nodded again, her throat tightening so much with emotion that she couldn't make an audible response.

"Now, don't let that tray get cold, baby. I mean, since it's from our cafeteria, it's already pushin' its luck."

Evvie exited the room, leaving Mary alone by her grandfather's side. After tasting a forkful of the meatloaf Evvie brought her, Mary determined that whatever animal they used to make it had died in vain. Still, it was the first thing she had to eat since breakfast that morning. Beggars couldn't be choosers.

"I wish I knew where you were right now, Geepo."

She glanced back at the window. Outside the snow was swirling like ghostly angels, a silent blessing over the coming night.

# 2

Joseph Connolly stood by the window in his mother's hospital room, staring out at the same snow falling quietly over Stamford. He couldn't help but wonder if heaven itself was dusting the earth with blessings—or if that was just a sentimental thought brought on by exhaustion.

His shoulders slumped under the weight of his responsibilities and gray stubble shadowed his face, aging him beyond his years. Though he was just fifty, his hair leaned more salt than pepper—a visible marker of the year's relentless stress.

It was just after eight o'clock in the evening and visiting hours in the hospital had been over for an hour, but they didn't pertain to visitors in the hospice unit. Joseph needed to make some phone calls but was hesitant to leave his mother alone lest she wake up scared and confused about where she was.

Earlier in the day, he had told both his siblings he was taking their mom to the hospital due to her shortness of breath, but this occurrence had become so common, six times in eight weeks, he told his siblings not to change their Christmas Eve plans and that he would play point that day.

It had been a marathon day at the hospital, starting with a

visit to the ER. At ninety years of age, his mother, Ann, suffered from age-related dementia. This affected her short-term memory, but her long-term memory remained intact, meaning that she was fully aware of who Joseph was and could name her other two surviving children, Peter and Christine. The three siblings thankfully all lived within a ten-mile radius of each other and traded off caretaking duties, though not evenly. More of the responsibility fell on Joseph's shoulders due to the fact that he had moved back in with his mother after his marriage had fallen apart earlier that year.

That morning, Joseph woke up to his mother gasping for air. This was the third time in the month of December that Ann's congestive heart failure had sent them to the ER. Fluid had built up once again in her lungs and while the typical treatment of diuretics and a high flow of oxygen helped manage her symptoms, Dr. Nora Anderson, the hospital's chief of cardiology, conferred with Ann's medical team, and they all agreed it was time to consider palliative care. All believed she was at the end stages of her disease.

Thankfully, Dr. Anderson did not use the term frequent flyer in front of Joseph; doing so would get his Irish up and have him unleashing a string of obscenities. She took a lot of his energy, but Joseph was fiercely loyal to his mother and damn anyone in the healthcare industry who referred to her as anything but a human being.

Joseph took a seat in the chair next to his mother's bed and began to wonder who was hired to design such an uncomfortable piece of furniture. Hospital rooms were unpleasant enough, why couldn't they at least have something that would aid in rest? He often joked that attempting to sleep in these chairs was akin to sleeping on a pile of Legos, though he thought the Legos would probably have better lumbar support.

As soon as he was mildly comfortable, his mother opened

her grey eyes and smiled at him—an innocent smile, the kind a child gives when hanging an ornament on a Christmas tree. Her silver hair was impossibly perfect, defying the bedhead she should have had after spending most of the day lying down. His gaze shifted to her right hand, where veins rose like a topographical map, clasping a round hairbrush. He knew a request for lipstick wouldn't be far behind. Ann Connolly always had a desire to look good regardless of where she was, including the hospital.

"Jo Jo, where are we?" she asked, calling him by his childhood nickname. "This doesn't look like my room. And why is your hair a mess?"

Ann Connolly never let her kids leave the house without being properly groomed. She couldn't remember what day of the week it was, but that did not prevent her pride from policing what her adult children looked like.

"We're are in the hospital, Ma," Joseph responded patiently, knowing it would be the first of many times he'd have to remind his mother where they were.

A worried expression came over Ann's face. "The hospital? Why? Are you okay?" At that moment, Ann wasn't experiencing any discomfort with her breathing and assumed that they must be there for him and not her.

"You were having trouble breathing before, Ma, so we came here this morning."

"I did? I don't remember that. I feel fine now. When can we go home?"

Joseph didn't have the heart to tell her that they wouldn't be leaving this time. Instead, he offered a little white lie to his mom, the first of many he'd tell that evening. "We have to see what the doctor says."

"Have I told you that I love you to the moon and back?" It was Ann's standard phrase of affection toward anyone she cared about—and any animal on four legs.

"Every day, Ma."

"Be sure to thank your wife for letting you take care of me. Is Debbie here, too?"

Joseph shook his head. "She's at home with the kids."

It wasn't a lie, but it wasn't the whole truth either. He hadn't told her they'd been separated for six months—he just didn't have the energy for the repetitive cross-examination that would follow.

"That's good. Being a mother to my kids was the best job I ever had. It's good that you let her stay home. What day is it today, Jo Jo?"

"It's Christmas Eve, Ma."

"Oh, is it? We must go to Mass tomorrow!"

"Yes, but if we are still here, Mass will come to us."

"You know what I want for Christmas, Jo Jo?" his mother asked, like a child excited to tell Santa what she wanted for her big gift.

"What's that?"

"For all my kids, you, Pete, Tina, and Mick to be all under the same roof again."

"That may be a little hard, Ma." Joseph cut himself off, deciding not to bring up Mick's death from cancer back in June for fear it would send them down a rabbit hole.

"When can we go home?"

It was only the second time he'd been asked that question, but Joseph knew it was a harbinger of what's to come and exhaled loudly to tame his frustration. "I'll go look for the doctor, Ma."

Joseph left the room and walked down to the nurse's station in the middle of the hall, hoping to find someone who might be willing to give his mother a sedative to help her sleep. He really needed to call his brother and sister but given the nature of the news he had to share with them, Joseph didn't want to be in earshot of his mother. He also knew that it wasn't news that could be shared in a simple text message. Hey, guys, Mom's dying isn't something you just send nonchalantly in a text.

Arriving at the nurses' station, Joseph found someone working the desk solo while his colleagues took their dinner breaks. He looked to be in his early thirties, his focus fully on pulling his long, wavy brown hair into a practical ponytail. Joseph didn't understand the modern fascination with man buns, but getting into a discussion about grooming choices was the last thing on his punch list.

"Excuse me," Joseph said softly.

As the nurse turned toward him, a few loose strands escaped, framing his face. His name tag said MANNY CARPENTER. Manny's brown eyes, warm and attentive, seemed to shine with a light all their own, momentarily catching Joseph off guard. He thought they were out of place in such a sterile place. He did a double-take when Manny's full face came into view.

"Mr. Connolly, right? Is everything okay?"

Joseph couldn't place the nurse's accent, Eastern European, maybe? Potentially Middle-Eastern? "Yes, no, I don't know. My mother is a bit restless."

"Room one-oh-oh-two, right? She is so sweet. You are a lucky man to have her for a mother."

Ann Connolly was commonly praised for her cheerful demeanor. If medical practitioners gave out superlatives, she would most certainly earn most likely to brighten a nurse's day.

"She just woke up and is a bit anxious. I was wondering if you could give her something to relax her or help her sleep?"

"Let me see," Manny said, looking through Ann's chart. "I see she hasn't had anything to eat yet. I don't want to get her comfortable until she gets a little something in her system."

Joseph shook his head. His mother had not had a full meal

11

in the past three years. Her appetite was nonexistent, for anything with nutritional value anyway. She always seemed to have room for ice cream, lollipops, or anything else that would delight a toddler.

"If you can get her to eat, I'll buy you a car," Joseph said jokingly.

Manny looked him over and saw just how tired he looked. As a long-time hospice nurse, he knew Joseph's own health was in danger unless he could get some rest. "When was the last time you slept?"

Joseph rubbed his face, looked at his watch and said, "I think I got a few hours last night."

"Tell you what, we have a light night tonight. It's only your mom and one other patient at the other end of the hall. How about I sit with your mom a bit and try and get her to eat and you just take care of yourself? You'll be no good to her if you are exhausted."

Joseph didn't know what to make of Manny's kindness. In the past, when he'd stay with his mother in the intensive care unit, nurses didn't offer the same charity. He chalked it up to them being overworked with caring for too many patients. "Are you serious?"

"Quite," Manny said, standing up. "And don't worry, I don't expect you to actually buy me a car after I get that lovely woman to eat."

The two walked down the hall to Ann's room. Hearing mumbling, Manny stopped right outside the door. Not wanting to interrupt a prayer, he held his hand up toward Joseph, using the universal sign for stop. "I think she's praying. Ahh, yes, the Hail Mary. It is a favorite around here, and one of my mother's. Did you know that most people at the end of their lives call out to their mothers, even if their mothers have been long dead? A friend of mine is a medic in the army and she told me that most soldiers, when dying in battle, call out for their moms. There's something so sad and so sweet about that."

Joseph shook his head. "Mom is very devout, but I think maybe she's talking to her visitors. She's been doing that a lot lately."

"Visitors? Is that so?"

"Well, not actual visitors. She's talking to people who aren't there. It started a few days ago. That same day, I found her in her closet reaching for her suitcase. She kept mumbling something about going on a trip."

Manny gently closed Ann's door, giving her some privacy, and turned back toward Joseph. "Her visiting hours have begun."

"What are you talking about? Visiting hours ended at seven. It's almost eight-thirty."

"Sorry, that's what we call it around here. At the end of their lives, our patients frequently report seeing loved ones who have passed before them. Any hospice nurse will tell you the same thing."

Joseph looked at Manny as if he just claimed to have seen the real Santa Claus leaving presents for the children in the pediatric ward. "My mother is almost ninety-one years old and suffers from dementia. That's all."

Knowing he wasn't going to make a believer out of Joseph in the hallway, Manny decided not to argue the issue for now. If he stayed the night, he'd experience it for himself. "I'm going to go spend some time with your mom for a bit. The waiting room is just down the hall and to the right. I'll come find you there once she's settled."

"I appreciate that, but I don't want Mom to think I'm ditching her. Let me at least introduce you and then I'll head down there."

Manny could tell that Joseph was one of the good ones. Some caregivers would simply jump at the chance to offload a patient's care, but he was different. It spoke to a strong bond between mother and son. "After you," Manny replied, gently pushing the door open.

Joseph entered and saw his mother pointing her finger toward the top right corner of the room, smiling and laughing. She looked over at her son with a smile on her face that seemed to impossibly brighten the room. "Jo Jo, you will never believe who just came to see me."

"I was only gone a minute. There's no one else here, Ma."

"Well of course you can't see him, but your father was just here. He looked so young."

Joseph was about to protest when Manny gently tugged at his arm and whispered in to his ear. "Do you see how happy she is?"

Joseph nodded.

Manny continued whispering, "Then don't argue with her. Whatever she experienced made her happy. It won't do any good to tell her she's crazy."

Joseph understood the nurse's point of view, even if he didn't agree with his assessment of what was actually happening.

"Who is your friend, Jo Jo?"

"Ma, this is Nurse Carpenter. He's going to stay with you for a bit while I go get something to eat. Do you want anything?"

"Oh, no, dear. I'm not the least bit hungry." Ann was looking at Manny, who was smiling back at her. "Oh my, is that a beard?"

Joseph turned to Manny. "I should have warned you, my mother mistrusts men with beards."

Manny flashed a wide, comforting smile toward Ann. "I can assure you I am very trustworthy. Just like Santa."

"Oh, I'll let the long hair slide, Nurse Carpenter, because you have a kind smile."

"And so do you, Mrs. Connolly. And please, call me Manny."

"If I call you Manny, you have to call me Ann."

"It's a deal, Ann. Can I sit with you?"

"Please, dear."

Joseph was torn between leaving his mother and going down the hall to call his siblings but knew he might not get a better opportunity and decided to head out. He paused in the doorway and looked over at his mother, who was still beaming with joy. "You sure I can't get anything for you, Ma?"

"I'm fine, dear."

"Go ahead, Jo Jo," Manny said, playfully using the name his mother used. "She's in good hands."

Joseph nodded and left the room, but not before hearing Manny ask, "So, tell me about your visitors."

# 3

Joseph lingered at the door to his mother's room, reluctant to leave but knowing she was in good hands with Manny. He crossed himself—a habit more reflex than devotion—and stepped out into the dimly lit corridor. The hospital felt like a cathedral at night, solemn and still, its fluorescent lights casting long shadows that flickered like votive candles on cracked plaster walls.

As he walked down the hall, his footsteps echoed faintly, each one feeling heavier than the last. He passed an empty room with its door ajar, the faint scent of antiseptic mingling with the ghost of someone else's grief. Finally, he reached the waiting room, its silence thick and weighty, like the air inside a church long after Sunday's final Mass had ended.

Joseph stepped inside, hesitating for a moment as though he were entering a sacred space. The room was sparsely furnished, its worn chairs lined up with the symmetry of pews. In the corner, a small plastic Christmas tree flickered with mismatched lights, its uneven glow casting restless shadows that danced across the sterile walls.

Down the hall, the faint strains of "O Come, All Ye Faithful" floated from a tinny speaker, the melody muffled and distant, like a prayer whispered from a kneeler and left to rise alone. Joseph turned to the window, where snow tapped lightly against the glass, weaving delicate frost patterns that clung to the pane like holy water droplets frozen in time.

He sank into a chair near the corner, letting out a long breath. The waiting room reminded him of the confessionals from his childhood—small, quiet, and suffocatingly still, as though the weight of a thousand unspoken words hung in the air. But there was no priest here to offer absolution, no light to signal the end of penance. Just waiting.

Thankfully, the chairs here were mercifully softer than the rigid contraption in his mother's room, and Joseph let himself sink into one, exhaling wearily. He was not looking forward to the three calls he had to make; one to each of his siblings and another to his estranged wife. He decided to start with his twin brother because he knew the conversation with his sister would be quite emotional.

Cradling his phone in his hands like a rosary, Joseph hesitated for a moment before finding his brother Pete's number and tapping the screen. The call barely had time to connect before his brother's voice came through, answering almost before the first ring had finished. "Jo Jo, how's Mom? Are you back from the hospital yet?"

Joseph took a deep breath, attempting to find the courage to tell his twin that their mother wasn't coming home, she was going home. "No, Pete, we are still here." The Connolly siblings never called each other by their formal names; Joseph was Jo Jo, Peter was Pete, and Christina was Tina.

Before he could continue, Pete cut him off. "What do you mean, you're still there? It's past nine o'clock! Why didn't you let me know?" Pete was quick to anger, just like their father, particularly when his stress level redlined. The Roman collar around his neck didn't put a governor on his temper.

Joseph had flashbacks to his father's anger and responded

17

the way he did as a kid when he was the target of his father's anger by remaining silent.

"Are you there?"

"Yes, Pete, I'm here. You are going to wake everyone up at the rectory if you keep yelling like that."

Pete was a priest and member of a religious community known as the Paulist Fathers, a missionary society dedicated to spreading the Gospel through modern media and fostering interfaith dialogue. He was assigned to a church tied to Sacred Heart University, where he also taught courses in modern journalism and social media marketing. Students called him Father Peter, but Joseph could never bring himself to use his younger brother's formal title.

"Like I said earlier, she was having trouble breathing again," he said into the phone. "But this time is different. The treatments aren't working and she's getting worse."

The voice on the other end of the call murmured something indistinct. Joseph sighed and ran a hand through his salt-and-pepper hair. "Can you please repeat that?"

"What do you mean by worse?" Pete asked, his voice calmer now, as if he had taken the time to realize the predicament his brother was in.

"I mean she's talking to people who aren't there. Dad. Grandma. Mick." He hesitated at the last name. The familiar ache rose in his chest, as sharp and cold as the wind outside.

"Mick, really? You know, today is exactly six months to the day that he passed away. Lord only knows how that's weighing on her."

Joseph thought that, for a priest, his brother really was a master of the obvious. "I know. I miss him too. Can't believe it's been half a year."

He reached into his pocket and pulled out a worn prayer card. Flipping it over, he avoided the gaze of the Blessed Mother and focused instead on the photograph of his older brother, whose blue eyes were as piercing in the picture as they were in real life. The Connolly siblings joked that they were his blue daggers, which could pierce the heart of any love interest he set them upon. Joseph stared at the picture for a moment before tucking the prayer card back into his pocket.

"The hospital cardiologist said there's nothing more they can do for her," he added, his voice quieter now. "They offered a hospice room and said they'll make her comfortable. That's where we are now."

"I'm leaving Fairfield right now. I can be there in a half hour."

"Isn't tonight a big deal for you? I assume you have Mass or something." Joseph had planned to go to Mass with his mother on Christmas morning, but that seemed unlikely. At least with a priest in the family, Mass could now most certainly come to them.

"I'm scheduled for Midnight Mass, but the benefit of being the senior guy here is that I can get someone to take my place."

Joseph glanced outside. The snow was picking up in intensity. "Don't break any land speed records. The weather isn't great out there."

"I'll be fine. And Jo Jo-"

"What?" Joseph said before his brother could finish his statement.

"Thank you for being there with her."

One call down, and two to go, Joseph thought. After a few taps of his screen, he was on the line with his sister Tina, who answered in an overly cheerful tone. "Ho-ho-ho, and a bottle of rum, little brother. What are you and Mother doing this fine Christmas Eve?"

The unmistakable sound of Jimmy Buffett's first Christmas album was blasting in the background. Tina was clearly enjoying her Christmas Eve festivities, which could either help or severely hurt this conversation.

"Let's see, Tina, we are spending it in room one-oh-oh-two at the hospital. How's the eggnog?"

"Wait, what?" Christina asked and left the room she was in, in exchange for somewhere quieter, a gesture that Joseph certainly appreciated, not being a fan of non-traditional Christmas carols, particularly those sung by a tropical troubadour.

Joseph relayed everything he had just told their brother and added that Pete was on his way.

"Shit on a shingle, why didn't you let me know earlier?"

"You think I'm not aware that you and Pete refer to me as the boy who cried wolf?" I was holding off to the last possible minute, hoping I would be making a different call. From home."

"You know, we also call you the angel of death, given you were there with both Dad and Mick when they died. Do me a favor, never come to visit me alone in my old age."

Of the three, Tina was the one who leaned on humor as a form of deflection. Joseph sometimes found it annoying, but he welcomed the joke at that moment.

"Yeah, well, this angel thinks you should probably make your way down here sooner rather than later and by the sounds of it, you may want to Uber."

"Great minds think alike, little brother. I'll bring some provisions." It was an Irish tradition that grieving of any kind be accompanied with some libations and Tina certainly did not want to be a traitor to her ethnicity.

"See you soon, big sis."

"Hey, have you called–"

Joseph cut her off. "Debbie? No. Not yet. She's next on my list."

"No, not her, though I'd be shocked if she came tonight. I

was going to ask about Loretta."

Tina was asking about their sister-in-law, who had been their brother Mick's devoted caretaker during his three-year battle with cancer. Her unwavering support during those difficult years cemented her place in the Connolly family. After Mick's passing, the siblings continued to treat her as one of their own, honoring the love she shared with their brother and the sacrifices she made for him.

"I don't know. Given it's her first Christmas without Mick, I don't want to open any old wounds with her."

"Little brother, they loved each other so much, that wound will never fully close. We can't not tell her. Mom loves her like a daughter."

"I know, I know, to the moon and back. I'll call her."

"See you shortly. Love you, little brother."

With two calls down and now two to go, Joseph took a moment to take a deep breath and let the reality of his situation sink in. His mother, whom he loved dearly, was going to die, of that much he was certain. It confused him that he wasn't as tired as he should be. It was strange; the exhaustion that had dogged him all year seemed to lift, as though some unseen hand was holding him up. On top of that, he'd now spent over twelve hours at Holy Family Hospital, yet didn't feel weary at all.

Perhaps this was a second wind kicking in. Joseph often managed stress by taking on as many responsibilities as possible. While Tina had humor and Pete had unwavering faith in God, Joseph used a punch list of things to do to deflect his feelings. His wife Debbie dubbed it a martyr complex. She was next on his list, and he swallowed hard before placing the call, as if taking an impossibly large and possibly jagged pill.

"I didn't expect to hear from you tonight." Debbie's voice rang sharply through the phone. "Figured you'd be at the

Hibernians, getting your Irish on."

Despite her maiden name being O'Sullivan, Debbie had always distanced herself from her Irish heritage—a habit inherited from her father, who'd been forced to take his stepfather's surname and resented every bit of it. Debbie, like her dad, carried a faint disdain for all things Irish, particularly the traditions and rituals of Catholicism, which she often referred to as "superstitious nonsense." It was a sore point between them in their marriage, one of many, and Joseph's silence on the other end of the line suggested she'd landed a familiar jab.

Joseph didn't take the bait. Instead, he got right to the point. "This isn't a social call. I'm just calling to tell you Ma isn't doing well and her time is short."

Debbie exhaled loudly. "Now, this is just great. Trying to ruin my Christmas Eve with another one of your mother's emergencies."

Joseph could picture his soon-to-be ex using air quotes as she said the word emergencies. "You were in her life for twenty-seven years; I just thought you might like to know. You are under no obligation to do anything with this information, Deborah." Joseph used the formal name she preferred rather than the nickname his family bestowed on her when they were first dating. His choice seemed to soften something in her.

"Look, this year with her has been such a roller coaster and you have been doing more than your fair share. Even though we aren't together, I still care for you. It just comes out in funny ways."

There's nothing funny about it, Joseph thought. "I'll let you decide if you want to tell the kids or not. Maybe not, so as not to ruin their Christmas." Joseph and Debbie had twenty-five-year-old twins, John and Colleen, who still lived in the family home while pursuing advanced degrees.

"They are in the middle of It's a Wonderful Life. Maybe I'll wait until George finds out how much he means to Bedford Falls before I tell them."

Watching that film had been a family tradition ever since the kids were little. It made Joseph happy to know that they were keeping this tradition going this year, the first he wasn't with them on Christmas Eve.

"Thank you."

"You know, I've often thought you were a lot like George Baily," Debbie admitted. Gone was the sound of the animosity that was present earlier in their conversation.

"How so?"

"Oh, come on, you've always wanted to get out of this town, see the world, and have adventures and I just wanted to stay here. It's one of the reasons we wound up the way we did."

"I'd lasso the moon for you, Deborah," Joseph said using his less than legendary Jimmy Stewart impersonation.

"I'm sorry about your mother, Joseph. Keep me posted. And promise me one thing."

"What's that?"

"You will take care of yourself."

Joseph knew that Debbie's saying 'your mother' instead of 'Mom' meant that she wouldn't be joining them tonight. He was actually relieved; he was emotional enough without her being there. Her presence might set him over the edge. He also thought it was better that his kids remain home, keeping their Christmas tradition alive. He wanted them remembering their grandmother how she was when they were little, not the senile woman who had been unfolding before his eyes over the past few days.

Next, Joseph mustered the strength to call his brother's widow, not that he ever thought of her as such. He said a silent prayer that the call would go to voicemail, but she picked up on the third ring.

"Jayhole!" Loretta greeted him, her tone unexpectedly light and merry, using the nickname Mick had coined for him years ago. "Merry Christmas. I was just talking with your brother."

Joseph's stomach tightened, but he said nothing. Was his sister-in-law suffering the same delusions as his mother?

Loretta, undeterred, continued. "I know it sounds crazy, but I swear he's still around. Sometimes, I can feel him. Like earlier, I was looking at the tree and the strangest thing happened—his favorite ornament, the little drummer boy, just fell right into my hands."

She laughed softly, a bittersweet sound. "I talk to him every day. It's my way of keeping him close, you know? And sometimes it feels like he talks back. Not in words, but little things—a flicker of light, a familiar smell, or that song we used to dance to coming on out of nowhere."

"'Crazy' by Patsy Cline?"

"Yes! He always said he was crazy for loving me. How's it going. How's Mom?"

"That's why I'm calling. They admitted her to palliative care this evening."

"I'm on the way."

"Look, I know what tonight is. Don't feel as if you have to come."

"I don't have to come, I want to. And your brother would insist. Oh my gosh, no way!"

Joseph got the sense that Loretta wasn't talking to him, but to someone else entirely. "Everything okay over there?"

"You'll never believe this, the Christmas tree lights just blinked. That settles it. Holy Family?"

"Yeah, room one-oh-oh-two."

"I'm on my way."

Joseph returned his phone to his pocket and took a

24

moment to let the gravity of the situation sink in. His mother might have her Christmas wish granted; all of her children under the same roof for Christmas Eve.

# 4

A soft knock at the door drew Joseph's attention. He turned to see Manny stepping in, a tray of food balanced in his hands.

"Mind if I join you?" Manny asked, setting the tray on the table by the couch.

"Not at all, but I'm not really hungry." Joseph realized that with all the excitement of the day, he hadn't taken the time to have a meal. Even so, he didn't have the least bit of an appetite. Stress robs some people of hunger the same way it does energy.

"You are in luck then; the food is for me. We nurses must eat, too."

Manny opened the tray, and the aroma of hospital meatloaf, mashed potatoes, and green beans filled the air, though it did nothing to stoke Joseph's appetite. It was still hospital food, after all.

"How is my mother doing?"

Manny swallowed the bite of meatloaf and washed it down with a sip of water. "All things considered, your Ima is quite well. She seems at peace."

"Ima?" Joseph asked, slightly confused.

"My apologies," Manny replied with a smile. "Sometimes I

slip into my native tongue. I meant to say mother."

Joseph smiled as he was about to get the answer to a question that plagued him since meeting the nurse earlier in the evening. "Where are you from, anyway? I can't quite place your accent."

"Where I was born and where I'm from are two different places," Manny said thoughtfully. "But I spent most of my life in northern Israel. Ima is a term of endearment for mother in my first language."

"It sounds beautiful," Joseph admitted, giving Manny tacit encouragement to keep using the term.

"Just like your Ima. Actually, she told me a funny story."

Joseph shook his head as he immediately knew what was about to come out of the nurse's mouth. "Let me guess. How my brother and I were supposed to be a large baby girl but instead she gave birth to twin boys?"

Manny laughed boisterously. "Yes, that's the one. And then she mentioned your sister's reaction."

Joseph stood up and placed his hands on his hips, imitating his mother describing what Tina said after two boys came home from the hospital. "Mom, if you were going to have two, couldn't one of them have been a girl?"

"She relayed that as well," Manny replied. "Were you able to get in contact with your siblings?"

Joseph nodded. "They are all on their way, but given the weather, it will be a while. I should probably go in and see Mom."

"Wait here a moment," Manny replied. "Your Ima is resting comfortably, and I have the sense that this break is doing you some good. It may be a good time to ask me any questions about what you can expect over the next few hours. There is nothing I haven't seen in this place."

Joseph couldn't lie, he was enjoying the downtime and he did have a ton of questions for Manny. "I have so many, I'm not even sure where to begin."

"I understand. How about I address something you mentioned earlier before we went into your Ima's room? You said you recently saw her trying to pack a suitcase for a trip, yes?"

Joseph nodded. "It happened the other day. Right around the time she started talking to people who weren't there."

Manny nodded, smiling reassuringly at Joseph. "This is a very common phenomenon for people near the end, before they start a new beginning. If you read through some of the brochures on this table, you will see it mentioned."

"What does it mean?"

"I can tell you aren't a very woo-woo type person, Joseph, so this might sound a bit bizarre, but I also know that you are Catholic, so maybe it won't. First off, a question. Do you believe in the concept of a soul?"

"I suppose I do. I mean, I was taught about that in Catholic school so yeah, I believe we all have a soul."

"Good, then this may not sound all that meshuga to you. At the end of our lives, our soul can feel when it is ready to depart the body and head back home to where it came from. So, it conjures up a story that the living person can understand. You see, the trip that your Ima thought she was going on is really the trip to the life that awaits her after her time on Earth is up." Manny paused to let this sink in.

"You were right about it sounding woo-woo," Joseph admitted.

"I know it is tough to believe, but we have seen this phenomenon time and time again regardless of race, gender, or religious background. It is quite common, and it typically happens when the dying person start seeing visitors."

"About that, isn't that just delusions of an aging mind? Or the results of medication?"

"It's easy to see why people would think that. But consider

this, not all the people we treat here are elderly and many aren't on high doses of medications that would cause visions. Your mother isn't on any."

"True, but she is almost ninety-one and has mild dementia."

"Let me tell you about a little girl named Kelly who was a patient here not too long ago. She had a brain tumor and nothing more could be done to save her life. A few days before she died, I found her talking in her room with someone who wasn't there. She was laughing and smiling as if she was having a grand old time with a close friend. When I asked her who she was talking to, do you know what she told me?"

"What?" Joseph asked, eager to hear the rest of Manny's story.

"She was talking to her grandfather who had just died a few months before. They were very close, and she told me how happy she was to see him again."

"She wasn't scared?"

"Maybe she was at first, but she told me he had been coming to see her for a few days, and he told her that he was going to take her home. She died later that week with a smile on her face."

"That story is both heartbreaking and beautiful at the same time. Let's just say, for the sake of argument, your ideas aren't completely crazy, what's the point of these visitors?"

Manny smiled, happy to see how engaged Joseph was in this conversation. "As far as dying goes, where do you think that ranks on the list of the scariest things someone can think of?"

"I read somewhere that research suggests it's number one, just ahead of public speaking for most people."

"Ha! Thankfully I never had to worry about that, my Ima told me I was born with the gift of gab. So, yes, we agree that dying is scary. Now before I go on, here's another question. The soul we talked about earlier, do you believe it lives on after death?"

Joseph paused and nodded. "I do believe that." As a practicing Catholic his entire life, the idea that souls live on after death had been drilled into him from a young age.

"Good. That will make what I have to say easier to swallow. If the soul lives on after death, would you agree that our loved ones can see us after they pass away, even if we cannot see them?"

"I have no proof, but I'd like to believe that is true."

Manny smiled. "Someone once told me that faith is believing in something even though there is no proof to support it, and faith comes into play here, so listen closely. Those souls who love us who have gone on before us come back when we are at the end of our lives to take away our fear of death. You see, if our loved ones are waiting for us on the other side of the veil, there is really nothing to be afraid of, yes?"

Joseph thought this was hard to believe since it challenged what he grew up believing about death and dying. He had learned that at the end of one's life, you died, went to Heaven, where you were judged and then you either were admitted through the pearly gates, went to Purgatory, whatever that really was, or went to Hell. There was nothing in the catechism about end-of-life visitors coming to comfort you. "All right," he said, "who gets to decide who shows up at the end of one's life during what I believe you called the visiting hours?"

"Now that is a big question, and the answer is God, and it is God who determines the circumstances of the experience, but I'm getting ahead of myself. That is a two-hundred level class in spirituality, and you are still a beginner. Plus, that isn't the biggest question on your mind. Why don't you ask the one you really want to ask instead?"

Joseph couldn't believe how intuitive Manny was. It was like the nurse could read his mind; perhaps that came with having been a hospice nurse for as long as Manny had been. "Fine, what happens after we die?"

Manny sat back on the couch, brought both of his legs up, and sat cross-legged, as if he was going into yoga mode. "Now this is getting good. You are proving yourself to be an excellent student. We have had many patients here who have had near death experiences, and I can share the similarities between those if you like."

Joseph nodded and leaned in, eager to hear what Manny had to say, believing it would comfort him to know what his mother would soon experience.

"All of them reported being aware of a separation of their spirit and body. Some were able to look down and see things happening in their room that they shouldn't know."

"Like what?" Joseph asked.

"For example, one person saw the unique measures a doctor was taking to save their life. Another saw their doctor leave the room, go outside, and get a drink from the vending machine. Neither should have been aware of these events, given that they were unconscious. That's how we know these experiences are verifiably true."

"Okay, then what?"

"Most people describe traveling through a tunnel, with a light beckoning at the end. Along the way, they often hear prayers—whispers of love and hope—from those on the other side of the veil. Then, they find themselves in a place of deep personal meaning: a childhood home, a beloved garden, or a serene field. What they all share is an overwhelming, indescribable sense of love and peace when they arrive. That's the moment when the life review begins."

"Ah, so that's when judgment happens with God or Jesus

slamming a gavel down?" Joseph asked, his question reflecting his own beliefs. He had been taught to believe that God, or some kind of judge, met souls in the afterlife and served as judge and jury for the soul's eternal destiny.

Manny shook his head. "Not at all. There's no judgment on the other side. What people describe is a re-living of key moments in their lives—times when they acted with kindness or fell short—and even feeling the emotions their choices evoked in others. But it's never about anger or punishment. It's simply a review, an opportunity to understand, to grow, and to see their life as a whole and what their soul has learned during its time on Earth. And yes, some people report seeing what they describe as a deity present, but usually one in line with their beliefs."

"Meaning what exactly?"

"Meaning that Christians see Jesus, Muslims see Mohammad, and Jews see figures from their faith, like Abraham or Moses. Buddhists, on the other hand, may encounter peaceful or wrathful deities in what they call the bardo—the state between death and rebirth. Importantly, these figures aren't there to judge. Their presence is meant to comfort the soul by appearing as something familiar. You're Catholic, so at the end of your days, wouldn't it be comforting to see Jesus?"

"Yes," Joseph admitted.

"Then that's who you would see, though if you would recognize Him is another story."

Joseph started thinking more critically about what Manny was saying and realized his only data points were from people who, while they experienced a near death experience, never really died. "This is all from people who have died and come back, right?"

"Unfortunately, I have no way of interviewing those who died and stayed there," Manny joked.

"Of course, but were they given a choice to come back? I mean, all of them were at the end of their lives anyway, so why choose to come back?"

"An excellent question. Yes, all reported either making the choice to come back or being told it wasn't their time to die because their soul's mission wasn't complete yet."

"This is the first time I have ever heard someone talk about a soul's mission. You make it sound like it was something agreed upon before they were born."

"Maybe it is, I don't really know. I'm only a nurse, after all. I just have a lot of experience with the dying."

"What's the difference if someone has a near death experience in hospice on a Wednesday, comes back, and then dies on Friday?"

Manny smiled again, a warm and gentle smile that unexplainably filled Joseph's heart with warmth. "Do you remember that little girl I spoke about earlier?"

"Yes, Kelly, the one who saw her grandfather."

"We almost lost her twice. Both of those times, her parents had us do whatever we could to save her. After the second time, she told her parents she was ready to die and not to worry about her because she was going to be with her pop-pop and that she would look down on them from heaven."

Joseph felt a tear fall out of his eye and run down his cheek. "Let me guess, the next time she coded, no measures were taken to save her life."

Manny nodded. "Kelly's healthcare team agreed with the parents that it was in the best interests of the child not to attempt to resuscitate her."

"So, what was her soul's mission?"

Manny's expression softened as he leaned forward slightly, his voice steady and reflective. "Sometimes a soul's mission isn't about doing something grand or monumental in the way we usually think. Kelly's purpose may have been something as profound as teaching those around her about unconditional love, courage, or even the importance of letting go. Her parents, through her journey, may have found the strength to face life with more compassion or to understand the beauty in accepting what we cannot change."

Manny paused for a moment, allowing the weight of his words to settle. "Perhaps her soul's mission was to remind us of what matters most—connections, love, and the peace that comes with surrender. Sometimes, a soul's mission is as simple and as powerful as leaving a mark on someone's heart."

Joseph felt another tear slip down his cheek, this one warming his face despite the chill of the room. "It's incredible to think that someone so young could have such an impact in such a short time."

Manny nodded. "That's the thing about souls—our missions may be quiet, but they're never small."

Their conversation was interrupted by a rap at the door. Manny and Joseph turned to see Fr. Peter Connolly standing in the doorway carrying a black bag.

"Ahh, this must be the other half of the large baby girl your mother was talking about," Manny said with a laugh. You two look almost exactly alike."

"I got the looks, Pete got the guilt," Joseph joked.

Manny got up and shook Peter's hand. "I am afraid I have been talking your brother's ear off and will let you two catch up. Take your time here and I will come back when I have some news for you."

Manny left the room, and Peter took the spot the nurse had previously occupied on the couch. "So, how are you doing?"

"It's been quite the day."

# 5

Looking over at her grandfather, lying so still, as if sleeping in heavenly peace, Mary couldn't help but think—though they were incredibly close, there was so much she didn't know about him. He had always been the rock of their family, but there were parts of his life he kept firmly to himself.

Mary never got the chance to meet her maternal grandmother, who passed away before she was born. But she knew that her grandfather's divorce had been tough on him, and it was a topic he refused to discuss—one of those family secrets filed under the "no-fly zone" category.

Once, after a high school hockey game, Mary had asked him about his childhood. By her senior year, she had already set her heart on becoming a therapist, and over a milkshake at the Shady Glen Diner, she decided to try the clichéd "So, tell me about your childhood" line.

Her grandfather had paused, choosing his words carefully. "I was the baby of the family, but that didn't mean I got a free pass. If anything, my mother expected more from me than my siblings. I was scared to death of disappointing her, especially since she didn't have it easy herself. My father wasn't an easy man to live with."

Thomas's gaze seemed to drift, as if the conversation had

unlocked a memory that he wasn't ready to revisit.

"You never really talk about your family, Geepo. Why is that?" Mary had asked, genuinely curious.

Thomas had smiled at her with a tenderness that Mary knew meant he was closing the door on the topic. "Some things are better left in the past," he had said cryptically, marking the end of the conversation.

In all of her coursework and limited therapeutic experience with patients, Mary learned that her grandfather was wrong about that. Leaving traumatic things in the past without resolving them could lead to all sorts of negative consequences, not the least of which was depression which, if left untreated, could lead to a whole host of outcomes including anger, addiction, and even suicide.

This was one of the reasons Mary felt it was so important to attend to her own mental health. Her mother and father separated when she was a freshman in college and, while she was well aware that her home life up until that point wasn't ideal, the dissolution of her parent's marriage had her questioning whether she did something wrong to cause them to drift apart. Therapy helped, as did spending time with friends who came from more stable homes. Their parents were examples of what strong relationships looked like and she realized her parents simply didn't have one.

Mary looked at her grandfather and could sense a change about his demeanor. While he was still fast asleep in his bed, she got the sense that he was really somewhere else, as if his body were present but his soul was elsewhere. She dismissed the thought thinking there was no way to prove it. Such a thought was even too out there for even her most spiritual professors, of which her graduate program seemed to have more than its fair share.

A soft knock at the door broke Mary's focus, and she turned to find Evvie standing in the doorway, holding a piece of chocolate cake.

"There was one slice left, and I thought you could use a little emotional support in the form of something tasty."

It's as if she's a mind reader, Mary thought. She'd been craving something sweet, and, lo and behold, something sweet appeared. Talk about the law of attraction!

"Just seeing that put me in a better mood."

Evvie entered and set the plate down on the table in front of Mary's chair. "It's amazing what a little comfort food can do. How you holding up, sugar? Your momma on the way?"

Mary had been in touch with her mother earlier, who had finally secured a ticket on a 6 a.m. flight out of Fort Lauderdale into Westchester County Airport. "Yes. If all goes well, she'll be here by nine tomorrow morning. Do you think it will be too late?"

"Too late for who, child? For you, your grandfather, or your momma?"

"All three of us, I suppose."

"Ah, well, in matters of the spirit, time isn't always what we think it is." Evvie's voice was gentle, like a soothing breeze. "Mind if I sit with you for a moment, sugar?" She gestured to the empty chair beside Thomas's bed.

"Not at all."

Evvie moved the chair closer, sitting quietly by Mary's side so she wouldn't have to speak over her grandfather's bed.

"In my experience, if he has the strength to wait, he will. But we cannot control the timing of the soul's journey. If his time comes before your momma arrives, he will simply pass on to where he's meant to be. The most important thing is that you're here, offering him your love and presence. That's the greatest gift you can give him in this moment."

"It's just that he had a distant relationship with my mom and my uncle, his two kids, though through no fault of his. They are pretty wrapped up in their own lives." Mary's voice was tinged with sadness. "I just want them to make peace before he goes."

Evvie looked at Mary with a warmth that seemed to radiate from her very being. "I can see you have a kind, compassionate heart, child. It's a shame that things are this way, but it's not yours to fix. In the end, what matters most is the love you've shared with him. As for where he's going, I can promise you, there's no room for anger or resentment there. Only love. Only peace."

"I didn't learn much about that in my religion classes at school" Mary admitted, "so I'm not sure if you're right, but I hope so."

"Oh, child," Evvie said, gently waving her hand as if to brush away any doubt, "religion ain't got nothing to do with it, not all the time anyways. In fact, sometimes religion can be a dividing rod between families. What I'm talking about has to do more with the spirit and the source of the universe."

Source of the universe? Mary thought. Evvie sounded more like a New Age hippie than a nurse at a Catholic hospital. "What do you mean, the source of the universe?"

Evvie's voice softened even more, her eyes carrying the weight of a belief she'd long embraced. "Child, what most folks call God, I refer to as source energy. I believe our souls carry a small fractal of that original source energy that made everything in this world possible. We're all meant to reunite with that source once we've moved on. That's the journey your grandfather's preparing for. He's about to return to the place he's always belonged, where he'll be whole again. He's going home, sugar."

Mary's mind was swirling with the weight of Evvie's words. She wondered how the priests at Sacred Heart would respond to such a belief. Yet, in a way, it wasn't all that different from what she'd been taught about God and the afterlife. She couldn't help but wonder if, in the end, it all led to the same place, regardless of the paths everyone took to get there.

"That's quite beautiful," Mary said softly.

"Child, I've seen more people cross over than I care to admit, and I can promise you this: your grandfather will be at peace soon. And when he's gone, watch for the signs."

Mary scrunched her brow in confusion. "Signs?"

"Signs, dear. After a loved one crosses the veil from this life to the next, they can send signs to let those still here know they're okay and watching over them. After my own momma passed, I'd get in my car after a shift here and hear a song that we both liked— even though my radio wasn't tuned to a station that would play it."

"What song was it?

Evvie grabbed Mary's hand gently. It was 'Wade in the Water', one of the songs Harriet Tubman used to communicate with those she was saving bringing to freedom on the Underground Railroad."

"That's beautiful."

I will be on the lookout. But what am I supposed to be looking for?"

"You'll know when you see them, baby. Now, you better eat that cake before it goes stale," Evvie said, standing up to leave but pausing in the doorway. "Oh, has Candace from social work been in to see you?"

Mary shook her head.

"I know she was trying to leave around nine to make it for the tail end of her family's Christmas Eve celebrations. She'll likely be in soon. Come find me if she doesn't show, and I'll hunt her down for you, sugar."

"Will do. Thanks again for the cake."

"Enjoy it, baby."

Mary placed a forkful in her mouth and smiled at how comforting it was. It's amazing how something as simple as a slice of cake can make all the difference, she thought.

Once again she found herself staring outside at the falling snow, now thankful she was spending the night in the hospital as the roads, no doubt, were becoming more and more dangerous with each additional inch. It's amazing how something so beautiful could also be so deadly.

# 6

Pete brushed some snow off of his shoulders before removing his hat and coat and placing them over one of the chairs in the waiting room. He rested his black bag on the floor.

Both felt slightly uncomfortable in each other's presence. The twins weren't as close as they had been growing up, though neither could really point to why. They rarely talked anymore outside of family functions, and it had been years since they could finish each other's sentences, a characteristic that followed them around throughout their childhood.

Fr. Peter Connolly was clean-cut and composed, in stark contrast to his twin brother's ragged appearance. Then again, the biggest thing he had to worry about that day was grading final exams for undergrads. Joseph had been tasked with navigating hospital politics since before most of his brother's students were even awake.

"How is Mom, really?" Pete asked, his tone gentle. The drive from campus to the hospital provided an opportunity for his nervous system to reset.

"Stable now. Nurse Manny is really great," Joseph said holding back a yawn. Realizing he was losing steam, he headed toward the coffee station, pouring himself a cup. The scent was bitter, acrid, but he took a sip anyway and immediately grimaced. "This coffee is penitential."

Pete chuckled. "I'll keep that in mind next time I hear confessions. Instead of asking for Our Fathers and Hail Marys, maybe I'll just have my penitents take a sip of that. Speaking of which, I brought my Last Rites kit," Pete said, pointing toward his black bag.

"Does Dumbledore know you left Hogwarts with that?"

Normally Tina was the sibling who would poke fun at Peter's calling, but Joseph needed a laugh, even if inappropriate, given how much stress he'd been under.

"Mom would definitely want the anointing of the sick," Pete retorted.

"Good thinking. The chaplain left early, given the weather, and won't be back until tomorrow. I'm glad you're here for Mom."

"I'm here for anyone who needs me," Peter said looking his brother directly in the eyes.

Joseph remained silent, a look of consternation coming over his face. He was, by far, the sentimental one of the family, a trait that his siblings relied on, perhaps a bit too much, while they powered through their own lives. He didn't know why he'd been unceremoniously elected the leader of the pack, but it didn't matter. He was the ultimate project manager of the family, believing that if not for him, no one would juggle all the balls it took to keep their mother safe.

After a moment, he drew up the courage to admit what he was thinking. "I'm scared of what life is going to be like after we lose her. I mean, you, me, and Tina barely get together on our own anymore. The only time we do is to talk about Mom or plan our schedules around her appointments. Once she's gone, what's going to happen?"

"Look, I know you have done more than your fair share and I appreciate that. But you have to understand, my schedule isn't as flexible as yours," Peter defended himself. "I teach full time, serve in a local parish, and have managerial responsibilities in my religious community. It's not easy for me to just drop everything at a moment's notice."

"Oh, so because I was fortunate enough to retire in my late forties, I should bear more of the burden for taking care of Ma?"

"I didn't mean it like that," Peter clarified. "I just mean that I have next to zero flexibility in my life. Why do you think the Church doesn't let us get married?"

"I always thought if they did," Joseph said, "we'd solve the priest shortage I hear about every weekend."

"Maybe," Pete agreed, "but I can't exactly drop my ecclesial duties because of a domestic issue at home. The call to single life for priests is just as much a matter of practicality as it is tradition."

"Yeah, but I still get the short end of the stick, don't I?"

Peter could see how frustrated his brother was and knew he was in a dark place. He reasoned if Joseph could share something vulnerable earlier, then he could certainly find the strength to do the same. "Jo Jo, did I ever tell you how I actually always looked up to you?"

This admission caught Joseph off guard, and he turned to his brother with a puzzled expression on his face. "You're serious?"

"It's fair to say that you and I were not the most popular kids in school, right?"

"That's an understatement. I think in grammar school we both got the superlative most likely to be picked last when choosing teams in gym class."

"Exactly. But you always had a little more moxie than me. I remember one time at recess, some older kids were picking on me. You ran right over without any idea of what was happening and got right in their face. They didn't know what to make of it and backed down."

"Yeah, I also remember taking one on the chin after school from two of those kids who ambushed me for making them look bad." Joseph massaged his jaw as if he could actually feel the pain that ran through it decades ago.

"Oh, yeah, I remember that. And when a teacher came to break it up, you didn't tell on the other kids. You just took it in stride. I never forgot that."

At that very moment, Joseph felt a welling of happiness starting at the core of his belly and shooting straight up into his heart. "You're my twin brother. I'd have done anything for you."

"And that was only one example. I've got plenty more."

"Thank you for sharing that with me, Pete. I guess I never really knew you paid attention."

"I did. And I know Ma did, too. It's probably why she expected more from you than me."

Pete's comment opened an old wound in Joseph that had been scabbed over by layers of resentment. Whenever there was a job to do around the house, Joseph's name was attached to it. It drove him crazy, but he just held it inside and let it fester. His mom took his decision to stay quiet about it as permission for the dynamic to continue. One evening, when Joseph was getting ready for a date, his mother asked him if he could go to the store and pick up some last-minute ingredients, all while Pete was watching TV.

"That one hurts, Pete. It drove me nuts that she always asked me to do things first before asking you."

"That's because I'd get angry at her, and she didn't want to get yelled at."

At least he can admit it, Joseph thought. "Do you remember the night I flat out said no and asked her to have you do it?"

"Oh yeah. She nearly lost her mind when you played against type. I remember the guilt trip she laid on you."

Joseph stood up and imitated his mother. "Whenever I ask anyone to do anything, they are always too busy. Well, let's see what happens when I'm too busy to do anything for you kids."

"It always scared me when she got like that," Pete admitted.

"Scared you?" Joseph scoffed. "It pissed me the hell off. I did everything and didn't deserve that guilt trip."

It was almost as if Joseph could see this scene folding out in front of him. Just then, he felt a great deal of sadness come over him, replacing the joy his brother had stoked in him just moments ago.

"I learned later why she was like that," Pete admitted.

"Care to explain?"

"Dad wasn't easy on her, we all knew that. Later on in life, she told me that you were such an ideal son that you literally were the answer to her prayers. When she thought she couldn't rely on you to help her, she felt lost and that's when the guilt monster came out. And here we are, decades later letting the same family roles play out."

Joseph appreciated what his brother had shared, but he still felt slighted. For all of his life, he was the good one. The one who said yes to everything and put everyone else's needs before his own, and now, at fifty, found himself on the brink of divorce and feeling resentment towards his mother, who is dying just a few feet down the hall. It was all he could do in that moment not to scream.

Peter must have picked up on his brother's feelings. "I'm going to head in to see Mom and she if she's up for the Last Rites. Given I will offer to hear her confession, you should probably stay here."

"Yeah, I have to meet Tina anyway. Listen, I don't mean to sound judgy, but the stress of the situation and all these old wounds are a lot. I'm only human, too."

"Of course you are. Do me a favor, though. If you do get to have one more conversation with Mom, be sure to let go of any lingering resentment. It will do the both of you a lot of good."

Joseph nodded and watched as his brother picked up his black bag and left the waiting room.

"See you in a bit," Pete said.

"No doubt." Joseph replied.

Alone again with his thoughts, Joseph felt as if the waiting room he is in was more than just a space where people go for a quick break or to have a private conversation out of earshot of their loved one. It wasn't a place of comfort, like heaven, nor a place of torment, like hell. It was somewhere in-between; a place for reflecting on the good, the bad, and the ugly of life. A place where unresolved emotions linger, waiting for absolution. It was purgatory.

# 7

Mary was in her own purgatory, caught between the land of the awake and the land of the asleep. She struggled to keep her eyes open and succumbed to the sandman's call in the uncomfortable sleeper chair placed next to her grandfather's bed. She had been at campus early that morning to put the final touches on a paper about codependency for her marriage and family therapy class and then had met with her advisor to plan the courses for her final semester.

After graduation in May, she was set to begin working in a supervised clinical role at a local mental health clinic, where she would accumulate the hours of experience required for licensure in Connecticut. She had it all mapped out meticulously in her master plan, which is something she had shared with her grandfather, who was always making lists and taking on various projects to keep himself busy. One of his favorite sayings was if you want something done, give it to a busy person.

Just walking through her plan in her mind made Mary's eyes droop and within a moment, she was sound asleep. Unfortunately, that's when the hospital social worker, Candice, decided to pay a visit. Mary heard the click clack of the social worker's shoes before she entered the room and was awake before Candice announced her presence.

"Ms. Mazzone? I'm Candice Bryant, one of the social workers here and want to speak with you before I head home for the night."

Mary rubbed her eyes to adjust them to the light and saw a woman standing by the door. Candice appeared to be in her early forties, with chin-length blond hair that framed her face in a way that seemed effortlessly polished. She wore a tailored outfit that gave off an air of sophistication, the kind that suggested either a very comfortable upbringing or a marriage to someone who could afford the finer things in life. Mary couldn't help but think that, in her experience, social workers typically didn't dress this well.

"Hi," Mary said. "I was just about to try and get some sleep."

"I'm sorry to interrupt that. Holidays are a busy time at the hospital, and I couldn't come sooner. This will only take a minute. I just came to drop off some brochures on hospice care, grief resources, and some support group information—just in case you find them helpful."

"Thanks," Mary said and put them down on the table by her grandfather's bed.

"I hate to bring up something so upsetting, particularly on Christmas Eve, but are you familiar with your grandfather's wishes for after his death?"

Fortunately, her grandfather had documented his final wishes in a book that he had handed to Mary earlier in the month. True to form, he had a funeral home picked out, had prepaid for his cremation, and even picked out an urn for his cremains. A burial plot had also been secured next to his brother, who had passed many years earlier. He didn't want to be buried next to his late ex-wife for fear that she might haunt him for eternity. The most intimidating request he had, though, was that Mary write his obituary and speak some words of remembrance at his funeral.

"He planned everything, so I am all set there."

"Wow, your grandfather certainly is a forward-thinking man. That's a real blessing. There's one more thing, then I'll let you get your rest. Has your grandfather ever mentioned anything about wanting to make peace with anyone from his past? Sometimes, at this stage, people feel the need to reconcile or share something that's been left unsaid."

Mary reflected on this question for a moment before responding. "To be honest, there's a big part of his life he doesn't talk about. He's always been very private about it, especially anything from before I was born. I've never pressed him on it, though. Whatever it is, I know he's been through a lot. He's always been there for me, and that's what matters."

"Yes, you are right about that. Evvie told me that your mother will be here in the morning. Is there any other family coming?"

"I was hoping my uncle would come but I haven't seen or heard from him in years. I put that ball in my mother's court. He's her twin brother."

Candice shook her head with disappointment. "It's not fair to put you in the middle of their issues. If you want, I can make some calls to him, just to bring him up to speed with what's going on with his father."

Mary shook her head, believing it wouldn't do any good. "My mom is the only person with a remote chance of getting through to him. If she can't, I'm not sure what you can do, but thanks for offering."

"I understand. Family dynamics can be complicated." Candice looked at her watch and saw that it was past nine. So much for getting home before dessert. She handed Mary a business card. "If there is anything you need, please don't hesitate to call, even tomorrow, Christmas Day. I've written my personal cell number on the back for you."

"Thank you. That's so kind of you." Mary accepted the card and put it with the brochures. After Candice left, she attempted to fall back asleep but sleep simply wasn't coming. She looked over at her grandfather, who was breathing fully and rhythmically, which was a good sign that, while his time was short, his passing wasn't imminent.

She picked up the brochures and glanced through them, but found little that she didn't already know. One focused on end-of-life dreams and visions often experienced by the dying, while another offered comfort to the grieving, outlining the Catholic belief in the afterlife. She shoved the brochures and the social worker's card in her backpack.

Realizing that sleep was unlikely to come for her again, Mary started to think about what Candice had said about it being unfair for her to be in the middle of whatever drama existed between her mother and uncle. She didn't fully understand why they grew apart and began to wonder if keeping secrets was a family trait handed down by her grandfather to his children. She vowed to be better at family dynamics than her role models were.

"You look like you are in deep thought, baby," Evvie said while entering the room. "I just saw Candice leave. I hope she was helpful."

"Meh," Mary replied. "She didn't tell me anything I don't already know."

"Is that so? Typically they help walk through what happens after, you know?" Evvie said while pointing at Thomas.

"True to form he has everything planned out. I just have one phone call to make after he passes."

"Well, ain't that something. Looks like he thought of everything."

"That's who he is. A master project manager who was an

expert at dotting I's and crossing T's."

Evvie smiled, realizing just how much of a gift Thomas was leaving for Mary, as no one wants to be in the position to make judgement calls on what they think their deceased loved one would want. "I bet you are just like him, aren't you?"

Mary nodded. "I'm grateful that I take after him and not my mother, or father, for that matter. I've got my whole life planned out."

"Is that so? Any room for a pivot, if need be?"

Mary shook her head. "No need. I'm graduating in May, then I will go to work at a clinic and within two years I'll earn my license. Then it's off to private practice after that."

"What if you meet someone, fall in love, and start a family? You can't have it all planned out."

"Meeting someone is not on the table at the moment," Mary declared adamantly. "I don't want to end up like my mother."

"Tell me more, baby."

"I was unplanned. She put her hopes and dreams on hold and then wound up divorcing my dad a few years back. Upended her whole life and now she lives in Florida in what I can only describe as pre-retirement with some dude she met on a cruise. I am not going to end up like that."

"Oh, baby, does that mean you think of yourself as a burden to her? Do you blame yourself for her life turning out the way it did?"

"How could I not," Mary protested. "She never lets me forget all that she gave up for me."

"Well, sugar, don't ever for a second doubt that you were the best gift she could have received at that time of her life. I know it may be hard to believe, but I look at you and see a child of light. That can only come from a momma who truly loves you."

"Well, you will meet her tomorrow. Tell me what you think then."

"Okay, baby. Can I get you anything before I go?

Mary shook her head and watched Evvie leave the room. Removing her phone from her pocket, she tapped open a music app and then thumbed through a list of songs until she found a Marian hymn that her grandfather loved, *Flowers of the Rarest*. She played it, hoping it would bring him some peace while he slept. The subtle smile that formed on his lips suggested it was having its intended effect.

# 8

Reflecting on the rare heart-to-heart he just had with his brother, Joseph hummed an old hymn his mother had always loved. His love for all types of music was something he'd inherited from her, and he fondly remembered singing this hymn every May during the church's May Procession honoring the Blessed Mother. Lost in the moment, he didn't notice the presence of another person until he turned around. Expecting to see Tina, his smile faltered in surprise when he found Manny standing quietly in the doorway.

"What was that you were just humming?"

"It's a hymn called *Flowers of the Rarest*. I could have sworn that I had just heard it."

"I'm sure you did. A young woman down the hall had been playing it for her grandfather just now."

Joseph smiled. "I wonder if I should introduce him to my mother. They have similar tastes in Marian hymns."

"My Ima liked that as well."

"Your Jewish mother appreciated a Marian hymn?" Joseph asked, somewhat surprised. He hadn't expected someone outside his faith to connect with a devotion to the Mother of Jesus.

"In the part of the world where I am from, it's not

uncommon to be influenced by all three Abrahamic religions," Manny replied. "The culture I grew up in was a melting pot of different traditions."

"How long have you been here?" Joseph asked.

"I stayed in that part of the world until I was thirty-three. Since then, my job has taken me all over."

Joseph thought about the ongoing nurse shortage in the US and how it had offered some with a bit more flexibility in terms of where to live, particularly in areas with more geopolitical stability. He considered mentioning it, but the hour was late and his mind was too full to dive into such a heavy discussion. Realizing he was caught up in small talk, Joseph decided to shift the conversation. "How's the patient doing, anyway?"

"We prefer to call them guests," Manny replied with a soft smile. "Patients come here to get well. Guests come here for other reasons."

"My mistake. How's the guest?"

"That's what I came to tell you. Your brother is with her now, as you know, so I thought I'd give you an update and see if you need anything."

"I assume no news is good news?"

"Well, her blood pressure's a little lower than it was earlier, but that's to be expected. I checked her lungs, and they're clear now, though I did hear a slight crackle. It might be a long night for you."

"Was she happy to see Pete?"

"Happy? Her eyes lit up like the prodigal son had returned. I take it she doesn't get to see him as often as she sees you?"

"He's very busy, so he can't come around as often as she'd like. Since I moved in with her earlier this year, I see her every day."

"Now, that's a beautiful thing—taking care of your ima in

her old age. I'm sure she appreciates it."

Joseph shook his head. "If she does, she doesn't say it. To be honest, I think she takes it for granted that I'll always be there. Story of my life, really."

Manny paused, letting the silence settle between them before speaking. "You know, Joseph, I once heard a story that stuck with me. It's about a man who worked tirelessly every day for years, tending to a beautiful garden. He planted, watered, and cared for it, expecting little in return. One day, he came across a stranger who asked him, 'Why do you do this? You labor for this garden every day, and no one ever thanks you. Doesn't it feel like a waste?' The man looked at the stranger, wiped his brow, and smiled. 'I don't do it for the thanks,' he said. 'I do it because the flowers are beautiful, and I take joy in nurturing them. What matters is that I take care of them while I can.'"

Manny paused and looked at Joseph to make sure he was tracking. Joseph nodded and Manny continued.

"The stranger looked puzzled, and asked, 'But when will you be rewarded for your work?' The man replied, 'My reward isn't here. It's in the way the flowers bloom, even when no one else sees them. The reward comes when the garden is in full-bloom, and I see the beauty in it that I helped create. And maybe—just maybe—it's in the next life, when I'm greeted by the gardener who planted me, He will say, 'Well done, my good and faithful servant.'"

Manny looked at Joseph, his eyes soft with understanding. "You see, Joseph, sometimes we're called to give without expectation. It's not about validation here—it's about the love and care we give, which may not always be seen or rewarded, but is never wasted. The true reward, my friend, may not come in this life, but in the next."

Joseph was speechless, as if he had just heard a modern-day parable that cut straight to the heart. The words lingered in his mind, challenging the way he had always viewed his sacrifices and the recognition he thought he deserved. He opened his mouth, but no words came out. For the first time in a long while, he felt something shift—a quiet understanding that perhaps he hadn't been giving without expecting anything in return. Maybe, just maybe, the true value of what he did lay in the act itself, not in the thanks he never received.

After a long pause, he simply nodded, the weight of Manny's words settling into him. "I guess I needed to hear that." His voice softer than before. Maybe Debbie was right after all—he really was a real-life George Bailey.

"Now that this is settled, I'm going to give you some time alone with your sister. I'm sure she's eager to see your mom, but something tells me she and Peter have a lot of catching up to do."

Joseph was momentarily confused—there had been no sign his sister was even at the hospital yet. Then, as if on cue, the elevator bell rang, and Joseph heard the unmistakable click-clack of high heels echoing down the hall.

Manny called out from the doorway, "You must be Tina. Are you looking for Joseph?"

"And my mother," she replied.

"She's speaking with your brother the priest right now, so why don't you and Joseph take a few minutes in the waiting room over here and I'll come back to let you know when she's done with Pete?"

"Sounds like a plan, Stan." Tina replied.

"My name is actually Manny."

"Relax, cowboy, it's just a figure of speech. Jo Jo is in there?"

Manny nodded.

"Great. Hey, you don't happen to have any wine glasses do you, Manny?"

"They are not something we keep in stock here on the hospice unit but help yourself to the paper cups we have for the coffee. Word of advice, though, don't drink the coffee."

"Yeah, it's penitential, sis," Joseph said and turned around to embrace his sister, who didn't disappoint with her choice of outfits. True to form she appeared dressed to the nines, looking every bit the glamorous figure she always was on Christmas Eve. She cradled a brown bag in her arms, the unmistakable sound of bottles clanking against each, other giving away its contents.

Tina hugged him tightly. "I'd say you are a sight for sore eyes, but you look like hell."

Tina's brutal honesty made Manny giggle. "I will leave you two to it. I'll be back when Peter says the coast is clear."

"So, little brother, red or white?" Tina said, removing the contents of the brown bag and holding two bottles up in the air.

# 9

It had been hours since Mary had heard her grandfather mutter anything close to a word; he'd been in a very deep sleep ever since. During that time, he barely stirred, yet she could feel his presence still lingering. He would react to the sound of her voice or the gentle squeeze of her hand, signs that he was still connected to her, even in his silence. She continued to wonder where he was; in a dream state or dancing between two sides of the thin veil that separates this life from the next.

Her body ached from hours of sitting in the uncomfortable chair, so she decided to stretch her legs. Walking over to the window, she gazed out at the snow, which was falling even harder now. Geepo would be overjoyed by the sight of a white Christmas, but at this rate, she doubted he'd be able to see it.

Her phone buzzed in her pocket, and she pulled it out to see a text from Tyler, a guy she'd been seeing in a complicated, on-again, off-again way. He was the type who appeared when it suited him, but when he wasn't around, he might as well have been a ghost. He was always too busy for her whenever she tried to make plans, yet if she ever asked for a raincheck on one of his offers for company, the guilt trips he laid on her could be almost unbearable.

Mary wasn't sure why she was even involved with him anymore. Perhaps it was because it was easy or perhaps because the thought of meeting a new guy was too much to handle, given all that she had going on in her life. If her grandfather knew that Tyler was stealing her attention in that moment, he'd dive into one of his dramatic lectures, the kind that always seemed to come at the most inconvenient times.

She could almost hear his voice, calm yet firm, as he sat her down, the familiar warmth in his eyes. "Mary, love isn't something to treat lightly. It's not about jumping in and out when it's easy. Relationships, real ones, take time and effort. You can't expect to fix someone or be the one who makes everything better—that's not love." He'd say this, always looking at her with that mixture of care and concern, like he was teaching her some kind of secret to life.

Mary had always appreciated the advice, though she couldn't help but notice the irony in it now. Her grandfather, a man who preached about love and connection, had spent much of his own life buried in duty and responsibility. He always gave to others, but she questioned if his own needs—his own emotional vulnerabilities—were ever fully addressed. He had never seemed to ask for help or lean on anyone the way he urged her to lean on love. She often wondered if he truly understood what he was advising her, and if, in some ways, it was his own unspoken longing for something deeper that had shaped the advice he gave.

"Love is a verb, Mary," he was fond of saying. "It requires action on the part of two people. Don't waste time on anyone who isn't willing to put in as much effort as you do in a relationship."

Now, with Tyler's text glowing on her phone, Mary decided to heed her grandfather's advice and ignore it. This proved a frustrating decision; Tyler started blowing up her phone, wondering why she was ghosting him. Knowing that a response would just set off a seemingly never-ending exchange, she decided to put her phone in Do Not Disturb mode and put it back into her pocket.

She could have sworn she heard her grandfather whisper, "Good girl." She turned from the window to go back to his bedside to see if this could be the sudden burst of energy Evvie told her could happen and got the shock of her life: her Uncle Jack was standing in the doorway.

"Mary?" he said, more a question than a statement, as he entered the room. "You're all grown up. I haven't seen you in so long I had to do a doubletake."

"Uncle Jack, you came!" Mary rushed over to him and hugged him tightly. It had been almost a decade since she'd seen him, due to some unspoken conflict between him and her mother.

"When your mother called me earlier, I knew it must be bad news. How long has he been like this?"

"Well, I brought him to the ER on Saturday because he was struggling to breathe, and they admitted him to the ICU because his vitals were so poor. After several tests, ruling out bronchitis, pneumonia, and any other respiratory illnesses, I got a call from his oncologist earlier saying that it is likely the cancer getting super aggressive and they recommended hospice."

Jack's face lost all expression, as if the years of estrangement from his father had just punched him in the gut like a blunt, unforgiving fist from a heavyweight opponent, a reminder of all the absolution they'd never shared. In that moment, he was immediately contrite for his lack of effort mending their relationship, realizing that he had allowed pride and resentment to block the reconciliation that should have come years ago. The weight of it hit him like a revelation, like the unspoken words he never said were finally being heard in the silence of the room.

"How is he?"

"This is his first night in Hospice. He hasn't been up since I've been here, and I got here late in the afternoon."

Jack walked over to his father's bedside and gave him a quick up and down. "My gosh, when did he get so old?"

"It's amazing, isn't it? It looks like he's aged twenty years in just the past few days."

"It's just that he's so frail. Like he could snap in half," Jack said, struggling unsuccessfully to hold back tears. That's when the floodgates opened. "Oh, Pop, I'm so sorry," he, whispered, pressing a kiss to his father's forehead. His tears fell steadily, washing over his father's skin as though they were anointing him with sacred oil.

"It's all good," Thomas whispered into his son's ear, but not loud enough for Mary to make out what it was.

"Did he just say something to you?" Mary asked excitedly.

"It was kind of hard to make out but I'm pretty sure he just said, 'it's all good.' That was actually his catch phrase after his great awakening."

Mary was super curious about her uncle's statement. "Wait, what's this about a great awakening?"

Jack gently rubbed his father's forehead and whispered, "Hey, Pop, it's me, Jack." But there was no response. It seemed that Thomas had drifted back into whatever state he had been in before Jack entered the room.

"Looks like he's back in la-la land," Mary said.

"At least he knows I'm here," Jack said and then took a seat in one of the empty chairs.

Mary did the same. "So, you were saying something about a great awakening?" she pressed.

Jack nodded. "Well, I guess you are old enough to hear this now. What are you, a senior in high school? That's got to make you at least eighteen, right?"

61

"Uncle Jack, I'm twenty-five! I'm getting my master's degree in six months." Gosh the dysfunction in this family is something else, Mary thought.

Without missing a beat, Jack attempted to recover through humor. "That was a test to see if you were paying attention. Congratulations, you passed." It was a technique he had picked up from his late aunt, back in the day. That, and a bottle of chardonnay a day habit, which he had put on his list of New Year's resolutions as something to address in the coming year.

"I know it's been a while. Honestly, it's okay, cut can you just get to the great awakening?"

"Well, in our family, we mark your grandfather's life in two time periods; PD and AD, meaning pre-death and after death. That man over there and his mother, your great-grandmother, had a sticky relationship, to say the least, but they really did love each other."

"So how did he change after she died?"

"Well, it wasn't really her death that impacted him directly. There was a whole bunch of other stuff going on back then. One of my uncles died around the same time and after Grandma died, Dad just became a different person. He started speaking up for himself more in front of my mother and, believe me, she never made life easy for him. For any of us really. At any rate, one day he declared he was going to start living for himself and start doing the things he wanted to do. Your mom and I were well into our adulthood by that point, so it didn't bother us at all. Honestly, we were too wrapped up in our own lives to have it affect us all that much. But your grandmother, let's just say it sent her spiraling."

"I never had the chance to meet her. I wish I did because all I've heard are the stories from Mom."

Jack shook his head in a joking way. "And let me guess,

you want to know if you can believe any of it?"

"Kind of." Mary laughed for the first time that day. "I mean, could she have been as bad as I've heard?"

"Look, I loved my mother dearly, but the woman could teach a doctoral level course in manipulation. When people stopped feeding into it, she'd move on to find other victims."

"Sounds like narcissistic personality disorder," Mary offered. She'd learned about it in one of her classes.

"That sounds right. I later came to understand that her father doted on her as a little girl and that likely had something to do with why she was the way she was, not that it really mattered. She dropped your grandfather like a bad habit, and he took his newfound freedom to cross off items on his monumental bucket list. That man did more in seventeen years than most souls will ever do in a lifetime."

Mary was intrigued. This is just the kind of stuff she wanted to know about her Geepo, especially since she was tasked with writing his obituary. "What kinds of things?"

"Walking the Great Wall of China. Studying with a guru in India. Hiking the El Camino de Santiago in Spain. And that was just the first few years."

"So why did he stop at sixty-seven? He had a ton of life in him just until earlier this year, when he was diagnosed with cancer."

Jack smiled at his niece. "I'll let you do the math on that."

A look of stunned comprehension came over Mary's face. "Wait, are you saying he stopped because I was born? Because of me?"

"You were his first and, it turns out, only grandchild. I think he was more excited about your arrival than your mom and dad were. How is your dad, anyway?"

"Fine. Still trying to be a TV scriptwriter."

"I see the strike didn't scare him. What restaurant in LA does he work at?" Jack couldn't resist throwing a jab at

Mary's father, a man he never believed was good enough for his sister. In Jack's mind, the only decent thing that man had ever done was provide half of Mary's chromosomes.

"I'm not taking that bait. So, when did Geepo start saying 'it's all good?'"

"It's so cute you still call him that. I have a friend whose daughter referred to her grandmother as Maga because she struggled to say grandma. I guess, depending on what side of the political aisle she's on, Maga either loves it or hates it."

"You have an inability to be serious for more than a few seconds, don't you? That's what my mom says, anyway."

"I guess she's right. Sorry. Anyway, he started saying it when he came back from surf camp in Maui. Yes, your Geepo took up surfing in his early sixties. He got in with some surfer bros out there who took a real shining to him. He started saying, 'it's all good' so much I threatened to put it on his tombstone."

"That is definitely not in the list of instructions he gave me," Mary said.

Jack shook his head. "A list of instructions? Why should I be surprised? Of course he planned everything out. The man was always a meticulous planner."

"I guess he didn't think it would be all good leaving his final arrangements up to you and Mom. Because of that, I'm the keeper of the green book."

"Green Book? Didn't that win best picture a while back?"

"Yes. It also happens to be the color of the cover of the book where he documented all his last wishes. I have it at home. I'm told we'll be needing it soon."

"Unfortunately, that's right, sugar." Evvie said, coming into the room with a couple of pillows and some blankets. "I saw you had company and figured this was that long-lost uncle you spoke of earlier. Took the liberty of bringing in some linens and pillows in case you are under the mistaken impression that you will get any sleep tonight."

"Uncle Jack, this is Evvie, Geepo's nurse for the evening."

"While that's technically true," Evvie said, "I'm really more here for you than for him. He hasn't needed me at all today."

Evvie set the pillows and blankets down and checked Thomas's catheter bag, where she saw no change in urine level since earlier in the day. "Not much urine production. I'm afraid his kidneys are shutting down. This happens at this stage. Has he changed at all since the last time I was here?"

"I could have sworn he muttered something to me before my uncle came in," Mary said.

Jack added, "And he told me something when I kissed him on the forehead."

"That's not unusual. He's drifting between worlds. Gonna be a long night, you two. Buckle in," Evvie replied. "Remember, I'm just down the hall when you need me."

"Thanks, Evvie," Mary said as Evvie left the room.

"Want to hear some more Geepo stories I bet your mother didn't tell you?" Jack said, settling into his chair.

"Nothing that might upset him," Mary warned, whispering. "Evvie said he might be able to hear everything we say."

"Who do you take me for, my sister? Heck no, these stories are ones that would put a big smile on the old man's face."

"Then fire away," Mary said and leaned in to absorb every word.

"Do you think that nurse has any Chardonnay?"

"This is a hospital, not a bar, Uncle Jack."

"A guy can dream," he joked and then began spinning some yarns about his father.

# 10

"Neither," Joseph replied to his sister's question about whether she should open the red or white wine. "I'm on the wagon."

"Wagon? When did you stop being fun?"

"It's the new me," Joseph admitted. "I was tired of waking up feeling like garbage every morning and knew that living with Ma would turn me into a full-blown alcoholic unless I stopped."

"Well, I'm not living with her, so I think I'll go with the white, which works because it's a screw top and I don't think they have a corkscrew for the red." Tina walked over to the coffee station, took a paper cup, and filled it with lukewarm Chardonnay. The grimace on her face after taking a sip suggested that it was too warm for even her.

Joseph got up, filled a cup with ice from the water dispenser, and offered it to his sister.

"Danka. So what's new with you, Jo Jo? How are my favorite niece and nephew?"

Joseph rolled his eyes. "At last count, they are your only niece and nephew."

"Which kind of makes them my favorites, gosh. So, how are they?"

"Honestly, they're taking to the separation better than I thought. They're still living with Debbie in the house, which I'm sure she'll get in our eventual divorce. Both had good semesters in their respective master's programs and are now at home, watching It's a Wonderful Life."

Joseph didn't want to talk about the mess his home life was, so he switched the conversation to their mother. "Don't you want to know how Mom is?"

"Hey there, little brother, are you accusing me of not caring about her? I just wanted to warm up into it, that's all. It's not every day a woman finds out her mother is dying."

It's not every day a man has to share that news, Joseph thought. Typical Tina, thinking about herself versus anyone else. He said, "The nurse says she's comfortable for now, but her blood pressure has dropped, and he heard the start of a faint rattle in her lungs."

"What does that mean?"

Joseph threw up his hands in frustration. He had a long career in advertising, not medicine. "I don't know. I guess it means that her body is starting to break down."

"When can I go in and see her?"

"You heard what Nurse Manny said. Pete's in there giving her the last rites. He'll come back when it's time to go in. You're stuck with me for a bit."

Tina went back to the counter where she had left the bottle of wine and filled her cup after adding more ice to it. "So long as we have this time together, there's something I've been meaning to ask you about Debbie."

"Here we go," Joseph said.

"Hear me out. I'm your big sister, and I need to know how to feel about it."

"Our separation?"

Tina nodded.

"What's your question?"

"Is there a third party involved?"

"Like, is either of us having an affair?"

"It's one of only two explanations that make sense to me. You are a great earner, shockingly charismatic for a Connolly, and one of the most attentive people I've ever met. Why would she want to leave all that? Unless of course either of you are sticking your fingers in another cookie jar?"

Truth be told, Joseph originally had the same exact question. Debbie's asking for a trial separation was so totally out of the blue he was still struggling to come to terms with it. He told his sister, "Neither of us has ever had anyone else. Maybe it was because I was married to my work for so long or spent too much of my free time with the kids and not her. Maybe she felt left out?"

Tina shook her head. "I don't buy that for a second. A woman doesn't leave a man because he's ambitious, successful, or overly attentive to their children. Try again, Jo Jo. See if you can figure out my other explanation."

Of all the times to grill him on his personal life, now was not the time or the place. "Okay, how about this, I'm too quick to jump in and solve everybody's problems?" He was being sarcastic. "And I'm too good at it?"

"Ah-ha!" Tina proclaimed. "You think you're kidding, right? But think about what you just said. Now, we are getting somewhere. Keep digging."

"Keep digging? Look, I'm not looking for any relationship counseling at the moment. Our mother is dying down the hall and this isn't the time or the place to take a Freudian journey on why my wife left me."

"Do you want to know what I think?"

"No, but I'm sure that won't stop you from telling me."

"Oh, how right you are, little brother. I think the issues you had with Mom growing up, playing the role of her go-to problem solver, set you up to find someone you could take care of. It's codependency one-oh-one. Tell me, when did you realize Debbie was manipulative?"

"Tell me how you really feel about her," Joseph said sarcastically.

"Seriously. I'll tell you when I knew. When your kids were born, you dropped everything to be there for them. It was you, parenting twenty-four-seven. Weekends. Taking them to playdates. Birthday parties. And she demanded time off for all that she had going on during the week.

"She was overwhelmed."

"There you go, still making excuses for her even after she leaves you. Do you remember that time the four of us— you, me, Mick, and Pete— took that siblings-only trip? Pete hadn't been ordained yet, and the trip was kind of like a bachelor party of sorts?"

"Nantucket. I remember."

"Do you remember why you had to leave early?"

"Debbie called and said one of the kids was sick and needed to go to the hospital."

"So, you left. And what happened when you got home? Both kids were fine, right?"

Joseph felt an anger stoked inside him that he hadn't felt in a long time, just thinking about that occasion, and others like it over the years.

"What a miracle," Tina said sarcastically. "She played you the same way Mom did. We all saw it, growing up."

"What you're saying is that I married my mother?"

"Yes and no. What I'm saying is that the dynamic between you and Debbie was toxic from the start. Now, let me tell you why she left you."

"This should be good," Joseph said, refusing to hide his sarcasm.

"Remember how you came to my house back in June after Mick passed, complaining about how Debbie was pushing

69

you to get on with your life, even though our brother just died?"

"Yeah. She kept saying how she didn't know how to help me and that I needed to get on meds or something to deal with his loss."

"Total narcissism. Instead of seeing your needs, she made it about herself, her inability to help you. Do you remember what I told you to say to her?"

"You told me to tell her that she isn't responsible for my feelings, but that doesn't make them any less real to me. And to tell her that I have the right to be sad after such a tragedy and that if it takes me a month, or six, or twelve to process his passing, that's how long it will take. I added that support is a verb and not just a word."

"Nice addition. What happened after you said that to her?"

"She didn't have anything to say. For once."

"Because you changed the script. You didn't rush to solve her problem. You clearly were able to state what your needs were for the first time in your marriage. And that, my brother, was when she realized the jig was up."

"You could be right. It wasn't long after that when she told me she wanted a trial separation."

"And be honest with me about this one, how did you feel after she said that?"

Closing his eyes, Joseph thought for a moment and a subtle smile came over his lips. "Relieved. I was actually relieved when she said she wanted to separate." Joseph immediately felt shame when those words left his mouth.

"Let me guess, you'd been thinking about doing the same for a while but were too scared to pull the trigger?"

"I knew she wasn't perfect and she treated me unfairly, but I thought she'd eventually come around."

Tina shook her head, refilling her cup. "Perfection should never be the goal in a relationship. Nobody, not you, me, and certainly not Ma are or ever will be perfect. We are human. But people like Debbie don't eventually come around on their own accord. They have to be pushed to see they could lose everything they hold dear unless something changes. And you, my dear, sweet younger brother, never offered that invitation."

"Invitation?"

"Yeah, I'm not a big fan of ultimatums. Giving someone a list of things that they have to address rarely works, in my opinion, anyway. Rather, if you share your truth and invite someone to consider changing, you have a greater chance of them doing something."

"So it's my fault?"

"I didn't say that, and, if you ask me, it's all working out for the best. You are the one who said he was relieved, remember?"

Joseph nodded. She could really read him like a book. "I guess you know me better than I know myself."

"It isn't rocket surgery," Tina replied, intentionally mixing metaphors.

Manny entered the waiting room just as Tina was making her final point.

"I love a good mixed metaphor. I don't mean to interrupt, but your brother is done giving your ima Last Rights. It's okay to go in and see her now."

"Ima?"

Joseph leaned into his sister's ear. "It's Hebrew for mother. Kind of his thing."

Joseph and Tina both got up, but Manny raised his palms toward Joseph. "She wants some time alone with Tina. More time for you in the waiting room. Plus, isn't your sister-in-law coming?"

Tina's eyes lit up, "You were able to get a hold of Loretta?"

"Yes, she's on her way. I guess I'll wait for her here."

Tina turned to Manny. "Care to escort me to her room?"

"It would be my pleasure."

"Well, mazel tov!" Tina said jokingly.

"That phrase doesn't mean what you think it means," Manny said, walking Tina out of the waiting room.

Joseph walked to the counter where Tina had left her empty cup beside an open bottle of wine. He lingered for a moment, debating whether to pour himself some. With a sigh, he shook his head and instead tipped the bottle over the sink, watching the last of its contents swirl down the drain.

Turning away, he stepped to the window and gazed out at the parking lot, now blanketed in snow. The cars, barely visible beneath the pristine white layer, seemed frozen in time. The untouched landscape felt almost sacred—like a purity, an innocence he hadn't known in far too long.

# 11

Joseph looked at his watch and saw that it was approaching ten. Given the lateness of the hour, he was curious as to why he wasn't the least bit hungry. What he lacked in an appetite, though, he made up for in confusion. Ever since Tina arrived, he couldn't shake the feeling that he'd been in this waiting room before. Additionally, at times he felt as if something were trying to pull him out of the room and draw him back into the hallway. Without a better explanation, he chalked it up to emotional exhaustion.

Thankfully, he only expected one more person to join him that night, his late brother's wife Loretta. After catching up with her and giving her some time with his mom, he'd join the rest of the family and sit vigil back in room one-oh-oh-two.

Joseph was torn about this pending encounter, though. He always enjoyed Loretta's company because the two were able to find something silly to laugh at even in the toughest of circumstances. However, they both missed his brother terribly and there was always a cloud of sadness in the air when they shared the same physical space.

Now, just six months after losing his brother, Joseph was in the same hospital where he died, about to watch his mother pass. "Why me?" he whispered to himself.

"Why not you?" Manny's now familiar voice came from the doorway, as calm as ever.

"How did you hear that?"

"It's a quiet room, Joseph. You'd be surprised at the whispers I hear in this place. So, tell me, why not you?"

Joseph ran a hand over his face, his thoughts clouded. "I was just thinking about the loss of my brother this past June. I was with him when he passed. It was toward the end of the afternoon, and we were taking turns sitting with him, his wife and I. She really needed something to eat, so I suggested she head down to the cafeteria. Not long after, my brother suddenly sprang out of bed. I thought it was amazing, considering he'd been asleep all day. He looked at me, and for a brief moment, it was as if he was himself again, like the old him."

"Yes, some of our guests do that just before the end. What did he say to you?" Manny's voice held a tenderness Joseph hadn't noticed before.

Joseph paused, his chest tightening as the memory surfaced. "He asked me to take care of her—meaning my sister-in-law. I told him I would, of course. Then he smiled and said thanks. And just like that, a moment later, he passed. I was so shocked it took me a minute to call Loretta. She sprinted back upstairs, rushed to his side, and threw her arms around him. The love she showed him in that moment, in her grief, it was one of the most beautiful things I've ever seen."

"Sometimes, our loved ones want to pass when they are alone to spare those they love the agony of watching them go," Manny said, his words carrying the weight of experience.

Joseph wiped his eyes, his voice thick. "Looking back, I understand that. There was this moment, just a few days before he died, when he was still lucid. He and I had a heart-to-heart. He told me things he didn't want her to hear—she'd just stepped out for a breather."

"Do you feel comfortable sharing that with me?" Manny asked, his tone still gentle but deeply open.

Joseph nodded, taking a breath before continuing. "I don't mind at all. Talking about it makes me feel better."

Manny smiled warmly. "I believe Freud called it the talking cure, and your people call it confession."

Joseph forced a small smile, his voice faltering slightly as he spoke. "Well, bless me, Manny, for I have sinned, and I've been keeping this confession inside for six months."

"I believe your brother Pete would now say something like, tell me your sins, my child."

This earned a chuckle from Joseph. "Loretta and I had been in my brother's room in this hospital for most of the morning. When she left the room to get some tea, Mick looked at me and said, 'Dude, I'm scared, but I can't tell her that.' What's interesting is that she had admitted the same thing to me earlier in the hallway."

"What, that she was scared of losing him?" Manny asked, his voice deepening with understanding.

Joseph nodded. "Neither of them wanted the other to know how fearful they were at that time. Their motto was 'I'm okay if you're okay,' so they both held their worries inside."

"That is both incredibly beautiful and sad at the same time," Manny said. "It's a reminder of how much we keep hidden for the sake of love, isn't it?"

Joseph sighed. "They were each other's rock."

"It's good to have someone who can be a rock in your life but sometimes, Joseph, we're the ones who need to lean on someone, too."

Joseph turned toward Manny; his heart heavy but grateful for the perspective the nurse offered. "Yeah," he said slowly.

"I've always tried to be the rock, you know? For my family, for my wife, for my kids. But sometimes, I don't even know where to lean anymore. I feel like I've been holding everyone else up, and now, now I don't know how to stand myself."

Manny regarded him for a moment. "It's okay, Joseph. You don't have to be the rock for everyone. It's okay to lean on others, to let them support you. This moment, with your mother, this is your time to let go of being everything for everyone. Be here for her and let her be here for you."

Joseph nodded, feeling a sense of relief flood over him, despite the sadness. Manny had unlocked something he had buried deep within him, something he didn't even realize he was holding onto so tightly. "Thank you, Manny," Joseph whispered, his voice thick with emotion.

Putting a comforting hand on Joseph's shoulder, Manny said, "Sometimes, the greatest thing we can do is simply be present, Joseph. Let your mother go but allow yourself to be free of the weight you've carried all these years. For you, and for her."

Joseph took in Manny's words, allowing them to settle deep within him. He didn't know what the next steps would be, but for the first time in a long time, he felt a quiet sense of peace begin to replace the tension that had plagued him for so long.

"I've realized you've uncovered a lot in these past moments, Joseph, but you didn't answer your original question."

Joseph offered Manny a confused look. "I've forgotten what the question was."

"You asked, 'Why me?'"

"Right, you and your superhuman hearing," Joseph said. "I was wondering why two people so far—my father and my brother—have chosen me to be present at the end of their lives. Now it looks like I'll be adding a third to that list. What is it about me that suggests I'm a grim reaper? My brother and sister joke that I'm the angel of death."

This caused Manny to burst out laughing. "Oh, I've met the angel of death. You look nothing like him."

Joseph thought that for a nurse from the Middle East, Manny had a bizarre sense of humor. "Anyone ever tell you that you say some really interesting things?"

"Oh, you should hear what they said about me in my hometown," Manny joked. "Seriously, though, someone choosing you to be there in their final moments is not something that should be seen as a curse. Maybe they chose you because of a lesson you needed to learn through their death. Or maybe you were the conduit between them and the other side. Only God knows. Tell me, you've seen movies where people die, right?"

Joseph nodded.

"And in your experience, does Hollywood get it right?"

Joseph shook his head. "Mostly not, except for The Notebook. That was a thing of beauty."

Manny smiled. "I'll give you that. To be fair, Nick Cassavetes had Nicholas Sparks' amazing source material to work with."

"Sparks is an American treasure."

"I agree. But back to the point, death in our culture is often looked upon as something to be avoided. As something bad. And sometimes that's true, in the case of a tragedy. But for people of faith, people like you, death isn't the end. It's a new beginning. Our loved ones are going back to where they came from. Back to the source of all that is, was, and ever will be. Your being present during their moment of transition isn't a curse at all, but one of life's greatest blessings. The question isn't why you? The question is why not you? Why shouldn't you, of all people, you who has given selflessly to others, have the honor of being there for your loved ones before their passing?"

"Flattery will get you everywhere."

"Enough with that!" Manny said, his voice rising with unexpected intensity. "I'm not flattering you. I'm telling you what I've seen. You are a good man, and you matter. I fear that you have a hard time believing that simple truth, so let me say it again. You matter. Every hair on your head and every cell in your body matters. You have needs that, yes, may not have been easy for you to express in the past, but just because you couldn't verbalize them doesn't mean they are insignificant. They are, and so are you."

Joseph was taken aback by Manny's sudden outburst. It felt as though the calm, compassionate nurse who had been with him all evening had vanished, replaced by a forceful energy—one that seemed to push through all the barriers Joseph had carefully erected around himself, as if Manny was clearing out the distractions in his heart the same way one might cleanse a sacred space of everything that doesn't belong just as Jesus did with the money changers in the Temple.

"You matter to your brother, Peter, who you've always been a rock for. Your example to him when you were kids made all the difference in the world for him. It's what inspired him to become a priest, do you know that?"

Joseph shook his head. "He never told me that."

"Well, he shared it with me. You also matter to your children, and you will most certainly matter to your future grandchildren. My goodness, you even matter to your soon-to-be ex-wife. The person you are becoming will inspire her to find out who she really is."

"How can you know all of this?"

"Joseph, I've spent my entire life healing people, not just in hospitals like this, but in the real world. In small villages, on the streets, in places of worship. And they don't always present with physical symptoms. Sometimes I meet people like you, whose emotional scars run so deep that they prevent them from understanding their true worth in life. Then the lies begin."

"Lies?"

"Yes, these people hear lies from others around them and believe them—that they are worthless, that they won't accomplish anything, that what they do accomplish is never enough. Damn those liars to Gehenna, for they are the true minions of the Evil One."

Joseph knew that in the Old Testament, Gehenna was a cursed valley outside Jerusalem, associated with the punishment of the wicked. Over time, it became synonymous with Hell in the New Testament, a place where sinners were sent to face eternal suffering.

"It means the valley of wailing," Manny explained. "Do you think you were put on this earth not to have a happy life? Amen, I say to you, no one comes into the world destined for anything but a life of joy. And that joy comes the moment you embrace the notion that you were formed in the image and likeness of the One who created you. And believe me, He knows that you matter for no other reason than you matter to Him."

A gleam came back into Manny's eye. "Since we started this off as a confession, I have a penance for you. From this day forward, I want you to live life to the fullest. Do the things you haven't done but always wanted to try, so long as you do not harm others. Find the joy that your Creator always intended you to have and let that joy be a light to others that inspires their own good deeds."

Joseph was truly surprised by Manny's monologue. "Honestly, and I don't mean to make this a joke, but that sounds a lot more constructive than saying ten Our Fathers and twenty Hail Marys."

"Well, as I told you earlier, my Ima really likes the Hail Mary, so say a few for good measure." Manny's friendly nature had returned.

A woman's voice from the doorframe interrupted their conversation. "Jayhole?"

A look of surprise came over Manny's face.

Joseph's face turned red with embarrassment. "Manny, meet my sister-in-law, Loretta. She used the name my brother used to call me."

"That's right," Loretta said, giggling. "His brother called him a gaping Jayhole."

Manny laughed. "Your family and its nicknames. Though it sounds better than Jo Jo. That reminds me of a circus clown."

"Mick refused to call him that, and thus Jayhole was born," Loretta said, going over to Joseph and giving him a big hug. "How are you holding up?"

"I'm fine, Loretta, but your ears must have been ringing. We were just talking about you."

"Is that so?" Loretta asked, whipping Joseph playfully with her scarf.

"I will let you two catch up and then I will take you to see our guest. Sound good?"

"Thanks Manny," Joseph replied.

"Thanks. Nice to meet you Manny."

Manny exited the waiting room and Loretta fixed her eyes on Joseph. "As a woman, I know that fine is a codeword for anything but, so spill it, Jayhole, because I'm not leaving this room until you do."

# 12

"Can I ask you a question that may be a little tough to answer?" Mary asked her uncle with a hint of trepidation.

Jack smiled at his niece. "You want to know why I stopped coming around, don't you?"

Mary nodded. "It's just that you were around so much when I was younger. What happened between you and my mom?"

Jack hesitated, his eyes flicking briefly to the floor before meeting hers. "You know what, I really don't feel comfortable answering that without your mother being here."

"Well, it's your lucky day," Colleen said as she stormed into the room, hair hidden beneath a Margaritaville ball cap and her sun-kissed skin betraying her Floridian lifestyle.

"Mom!" Mary jumped to hug her mother. "I thought you couldn't get here 'til morning."

"Yeah, well, I've been trying to reach you all evening. My calls kept going to voicemail. I had an epiphany to try airports other than Fort Lauderdale and was able to get a flight out of West Palm.

Colleen and Jack locked eyes, the weight of years of estrangement hanging between them. For a moment, it felt as though time itself paused, a silent standoff as they both held their ground. Then, almost as if the dam had broken, they each moved forward in unspoken understanding, rushing to embrace one another as if trying to make up for all the lost time in one gesture.

While they hugged it out, Mary dug her phone from her pocket, glancing at the screen. Sure enough, her mother's texts were there, along with double the number of messages from Tyler—the reason she'd put her phone on do-not-disturb in the first place.

"How's he doing?" Colleen asked, pointing to her father.

"Same as he's been all day," Mary said, "but maybe you'll stir something in him. He perked up when Uncle Jack arrived."

Colleen nodded and slowly approached the bedside. Leaning over, she kissed her father's veiny hand and whispered into his ear, "It's Col Col, Daddy. I'm here."

For a moment, nothing happened. Then, just as they were about to lose hope, Thomas gently squeezed her hand, his faint voice breaking the silence. "To the moon and back."

Mary rushed to the bed. "Did he just say something? Geepo, are you there?"

"Dad, it's me, Jack. Can you hear me?"

The three of them watched as Thomas offered a slight nod, then slipped back into whatever state he had been in.

"Looks like he's back in la-la land," Mary said softly.

"At least he knows we're here," Colleen replied, taking a seat beside her daughter. "You were asking Jack about the falling out between us?"

"I had just finished telling Mary about dad's post-midlife crisis," Jack said.

Colleen started to put her own spin on the story. "Yes, after Grandma and Uncle Michael passed, he became a completely different person. It was like something clicked for him."

Mary furrowed her brow. "What do you think happened?"

"Their deaths hit him very hard. I honestly thought we were going to lose him, but then—he just changed. Completely. It was like he came alive. You remember, Jack? We were in our mid-twenties."

"We were twenty-five, exactly," Jack added, a nostalgic smile tugging at his lips. "Exactly the age you are now, Mary. That's when Dad started checking things off his bucket list. Travel, adventure. Heck, he even changed his name."

Colleen shook her head with the last revelation.

Mary's eyes widened. "Wait, Thomas isn't his real name?"

"Well," Jack said with a laugh, "to be accurate, he didn't change his name so much as embrace his given name. You see, he was named Thomas after his father. To avoid any confusion in the house, his parents referred to him by his middle name. After his 'great awakening' as we called it, he started using Thomas publicly, to symbolize his new beginning."

"That must have been confusing for you, right?"

"Well, not for us," Jack replied. "We just kept always calling him Dad."

"That solves that mystery," Mary observed, "but what about the rift between you two?"

Jack looked over at his sister. "Now for the hard truths. You want to take this, sis?"

"Your uncle never got over the fact that I moved to Florida after divorcing your father when you went off to college."

"Oh, c'mon, sis, it was more than that," Jack protested.

"I guess you could say I took a page out of his playbook." Colleen pointed to her father.

"You mean you had a great awakening, too?" Mary asked.

"In a way, yes. Look, there was a period of time when I was in love with your father and then I wasn't. We were high school sweethearts, and that romance followed us to college and then we got married right after graduation."

"Yeah, they were a regular Brenda and Eddie," Jack joked, referencing a Billy Joel song.

"When your grandfather started to see the holes in our marital ship, he sat me down for a tough heart-to-heart. He convinced me that the best thing I could do for you is to show you a happier version of me."

"So that's why you left Dad? For me?" Mary protested. "That's bull, Mom."

"No, I did it for me. But it came with the benefit of being an example of what a strong woman should be for her daughter."

"Yeah, and then that strong woman up and moved to Florida," Jack offered.

"Your uncle is just bitter because he missed me so much," Coleen said. "I mean, we weren't kids anymore. We both had our own lives."

"So what of it?" Jack protested. "Not only were you my best friend, but you were leaving me all alone to take care of Dad in his golden years."

Mary coughed. "Excuse me, but what am I, chopped liver? I'm the one who has gladly been taking care of Geepo, your father, while you both have been remarkably absent in his life. And mine, too. Am I understanding all of this correctly?"

"Sounds right," Coleen and Jack said in unison, the same way they did when they were kids.

Mary could really take charge when she needed to and she felt this was the time. "Now it's time for each of you to put your big kid pants on, admit that you were both wrong, and make up, because one, that's what he would have wanted and two, he doesn't have a lot of time left."

Jack looked at his sister. "Sorry, Col Col."

"Truce, Jack Jack?"

Coleen hugged her brother and turned around to address her daughter. "You know, you are a lot like him."

"Like Geepo? How?"

"For one, he was the anchor of the family, keeping us all grounded when the storms were raging around us. And you have done the same throughout his illness all the while kicking butt in your graduate program."

"It's not like I had a choice, Mom," Mary said, with a hint of resentment in her tone. "You were wasting away in Margaritaville with what's-his-bucket, while Uncle Jack over here was, well, I have no idea what he was doing because he stopped coming around."

"His name is Mac and I know I haven't been perfect..." Colleen started to protest, but a wave of Mary's hand cut her off.

"I don't expect perfection, but there is a fine line between living for yourself and ignoring your only child. Do you know that I'm graduating this May? I mean, heck, Uncle Jack thought I was still in high school."

"I told you that was a test," Jack said defensively.

Mary and Colleen flashed him a look suggesting that continuing to use humor as a defense mechanism was futile.

"Okay, jeez, mea culpa," Jack offered.

"I'm sorry if I'm coming across bitchy, but the stress of this situation is finally hitting me and I'm about to lose the one constant presence in my life since I can remember. So please, give me a little space."

Mary sprang from her chair and darted out the door leaving the two siblings sitting in the silence of their father's hospice room. They knew enough not to go after her and that she, of all people, deserved some time to cool off. They knew they deserved exactly what she just verbally served them.

# 13

"It's hard for me to explain it, Loretta, but ever since I came into this waiting room, I've just felt off," Joseph said, responding to his sister-in-law's observation that saying one is fine usually means anything but.

"Take a deep breath and try to put some words around how you feel. I know this has been hard for you to do in the past, but give it a go now."

Joseph closed his eyes and took in a few deep breaths to center himself. He reflected on his memory of the day; coming to the hospital with his mother, getting her settled in a hospice room, meeting Manny, and then settling into this waiting room, where he caught up with both Pete and Tina.

"Okay, this is going to sound crazy, but ever since I came into this room, I've had the feeling like I've been here before."

"Maybe it's déjà vu?"

"Yes, but when I've experienced that in the past, it would last for a fleeting second. This has been going on ever since I've been here."

"Interesting," Loretta said. "What were you doing right before you came in here?"

"I was with Mom in her room. I had just introduced her to Nurse Manny and once I saw she was comfortable with him,

I came down here. But you want to know what's crazy?"

"Why stop telling me now?" Loretta joked.

"When I was talking with both Pete and Tina earlier, something felt off."

"Off how?"

"Like, it shouldn't have happened that way. Or that it didn't happen that way."

"What do you mean didn't happen that way? How is that possible?"

"I don't know!" Joseph said, frustrated. "It's hard to explain. It's like I kind of remember being here before but it didn't feel right that they were actually there because..." he tapped his hand to his head, as if that would jar his memories.

"Yes?" Loretta said eagerly, hoping he'd been able to connect the dots about what this experience really was all about.

The blood seemed to drain from Joseph's face when the realization hit him. "Because they weren't here for my mom. You aren't here for her either, are you?"

Loretta shook her head.

Joseph felt unsteady on his feet and plunged down onto the couch. "Which means you are all here for me?"

Loretta nodded. "Joseph, there's a reason why I'm the last one here for you but it's going to take a little time to explain."

"Hold a second." Joseph got up from the couch and darted out of the waiting room. He sprinted down the hallway until he reached room one-oh-oh-two. Inside, he found an empty room, with no sign that any guests had been there that day. Loretta appeared in the doorway.

"My mother was here earlier today. I saw her with my own eyes."

"You are partly right. Your mother was in this room, but that was forty-two years ago."

Joseph's eyes went wide. "Okay, I thought I was the crazy one. If my mother died forty-two years ago, that would make me what, ninety-two? Look at me Loretta, I'm fifty years old."

"Are you sure about that? Look in that mirror," Loretta said pointing out a mirror above the end table adjacent to the bed.

Joseph did as she suggested, and his mouth practically dropped to the floor when he saw the face of a very old man staring at him. He immediately put his hands on his face to make sure he wasn't dreaming. Satisfied that he wasn't, he walked out of the room and back down the hall toward the waiting room.

As Joseph entered, he noticed a subtle change in the room. In addition to the doorway, he had just walked through, there was another one in the corner—one he hadn't seen before. He approached it and tried the handle, only to find it locked.

"That is not available to you yet, Thomas."

"Thomas?" Joseph was confused. Why did his sister-in-law call him by the wrong name? "Why did you call me that? No one calls me that."

"This is a lot to handle right now but try and center yourself again and think about it. Think about your life after your mother died. After the divorce from Debbie. Try and call up those memories."

Joseph did and received a download of so much information it practically knocked him off his feet. He had to grab onto Loretta's shoulders just to maintain his balance.

"My goodness. I do go by Thomas now and I am ninety-two. I have two grown adult children. Debbie has passed on. Pete and Tina are both gone and I have a... granddaughter?"

"Yes, Mary. She's not far from us right now."

Joseph walked over to the couch and took a seat. Loretta did the same. "So can you explain to me what's going on?

What's the purpose of me reliving the night my mom died?"

"You didn't exactly relive the night she died because on that actual night, you were all alone, weren't you?"

"Kind of," Joseph agreed. "Pete and Tina didn't make it in time. The only person who was with me was my mom's nurse, Evvie. She was one of the most caring and insightful people I've ever met."

"Believe it or not, she still works here and she is your nurse tonight."

Joseph took another minute to reflect. "Cancer. I have cancer, that's right. And my granddaughter took me to Holy Family Hospital a few days ago. So, wait, now that I remember that Evvie was my nurse when mom died, who is Manny?"

"An excellent question," Manny said in his soft Middle-Eastern accented voice. "I thought my choice of name was pretty on the nose, but you've been a little slow on the uptake. Don't worry about it, it's very common."

Joseph's eyes looked upward and then shifted from left to right multiple times, trying to process what Manny meant by on the nose. "Manny Carpenter," he said out loud.

"Manny Carpenter," Loretta repeated, hoping Joseph would figure it out.

Seeing he was struggling, Manny said, "Emmanuel Carpenter," and then started singing, "Oh come, oh come, Emmanuel, and ransom captive Israel." He then whispered into Loretta's ear, "By the way, I'm the Emmanuel they are singing about in that hymn."

"I know that. He's the one who hasn't figured it out yet," Loretta replied.

"Jesus? This entire time this afternoon I've been in your presence, but I didn't recognize you?"

"To be fair, we've never met in person since you've been down here. My own followers didn't recognize me after I came back from the dead. You win some, you lose some."

"You are a lot funnier than I imagined."

"I had the same reaction during my life review," Loretta said.

"Your Life review?" Joseph asked. "You mean, you're…? Was that what I was experiencing today, a life review?"

"I hinted at it before when you thought we were talking about your mother," Manny said with a wry smile. "The Creator of the universe did not put you all here to be miserable. Laughter and joy were a big part of my ministry up until the very end. Without laughter and joy, how do you think I was able to attract so many followers? Fear doesn't work that way, not long term anyway."

"Please tell me this then," Joseph said, "what was the point of bringing me back to the night my mother died and using that as the setting for my review?"

"Now that is a smart question, isn't it, Loretta?"

"I agree, but I think you should tell him, Manny."

"It's almost like you two have rehearsed this," Joseph said.

"The night your mother died was the biggest turning point in your life. After that, you decided to live for yourself. The very next day, you put that bucket list together and started crossing items off if it. In a sense, you were reborn that day. So, Spirit decided to bring you back to the point not of your mother's death, but of your first death. It wasn't arbitrary."

"Back then, I was still reeling over my brother Mick's passing. Shortly after that, my wife asked for a separation, and then Mom got sick. I honestly thought I'd be next, but I have to tell you, after having a dark night of the soul the night she passed, I decided to make some big changes in my life. Actually, Evvie the nurse was the one who really helped me see the opportunities I had in front of me."

"Go back to that dark night for a moment," Manny said. "It happened right in this room, do you remember?"

"Yes, now I do. This is where I made the phone calls to Pete, Tina, Debbie, and Loretta, didn't I? That's what threw me earlier. All of those happened the way they did in this life review. The only thing different was that tonight, most of them showed up."

"That's right," Manny affirmed, "their conversations with you were your life review. Remember how I told you that you would feel the emotions you evoked in others?"

Joseph nodded. "And I did. But why didn't I experience anything after I was fifty?"

"The night is still young," Manny said, smiling. "You will have one more room to go to, and it's not the one on the other side of that door." Manny pointed to the door that Joseph saw when he first came back into the waiting room.

"I guess that means I have to go back to my room," Joseph reasoned.

Manny nodded.

"But this is so peaceful here. This is the first time I can remember in years that I haven't felt any pain. All of my thoughts are clear. Can't I just stay here?"

"Your time for waiting will soon be at an end," Manny replied, "but this room has served its purpose for now. There are some people who you need to see."

"Come, Jayhole, I'll be there with you."

Joseph looked at Loretta. She still had the face of an angel, so much so that his brother Mick had nicknamed her Angelica when they were dating. "Why haven't I seen my brother tonight?"

"As Manny said, the night is still young. Are you ready?"

Loretta extended her arm and Joseph put his through it. He then turned to Manny and asked, "Are you coming?"

"Joseph, I've never left you."

Together, the three of them exited the waiting room and made their way down the hall to room one-oh-two-oh, where

Joseph saw his twins Jack and Colleen sitting in chairs and granddaughter Mary praying by his bedside. Joseph could hear the prayer in his own ears, the Hail Mary.

"Now I know why you said your mother liked that one so much."

"Again, I was pretty on the nose with the references," Manny said, smiling.

"They can't see us, right?"

Manny shook his head. "Just like in A Christmas Carol."

"How do I get back into my body?"

"Just imagine it, and it will be," Manny replied.

"It's that simple?"

"If you call that simple," Loretta joked.

"Do I have to?"

"You have no choice," Manny said.

Joseph closed his eyes, tried to imagine himself back in his body, and felt something shift inside him. It's as if he went from being free to move about time and space and then being once again confined to an extremely tight spot. He was so uncomfortable he started to squirm like a fish that had just been caught and found itself on the deck of a boat. A sense of panic welled up inside him and he sprang up from the waist clutching his throat and took a deep breath.

"Dad?" he heard a pretty voice say.

"Pop? an excited voice said. This one belonged to a man.

"Geepo?" He heard yet another voice and immediately knew it was Mary's.

It took a lot of energy, but he opened his eyes and saw his children and granddaughter looking at him with a mixture of hope and bewilderment.

# 14

At 11:53, just seven minutes before Christmas Eve would become Christmas Day, and much to the surprise of everyone in his room, Thomas Joseph Connolly sprang up in bed and opened his eyes. The first person he saw was his granddaughter, Mary. Then, his adult twins, Jack and Colleen came into focus. He heard them call out at once, "Dad, Pop, Geepo."

Realizing he needed to catch his breath, Thomas held his hand up, the universal sign for 'please give me a minute.'

After filling his lungs a few times with some deep breaths, Thomas attempted to speak, but his words were inaudible. His voice crackled at first because his throat was dry from not having anything to drink in at least twelve hours.

Mary poured some water for him into a small cup from the pitcher by his bedside. She held onto the cup and gently placed the straw in his mouth. "Have a few sips, Geepo."

Thomas drank some water and thought it was, by far, the best he'd ever tasted. He attempted to speak once more, this time with success.

"I'm so happy to see you all here. This is the best Christmas present I could have ever received. I'm sure you have some questions for me, but my time is limited and there is so much I need to share with you. Mary, you may want to record this on that phone of yours, just don't answer any texts from Tyler."

"Tyler?" Colleen asked her daughter.

"Some asshat. I'll tell you later," Mary replied with a whisper, hoping her grandfather didn't hear her choice of language.

"Life is too short to deal with asshats, Mary," Thomas said. "And that's just one of the messages I have for you."

After taking another sip, Thomas continued. "I can't tell you everything I've experienced during the past day because it would take up way too much time and you wouldn't believe me anyway. Instead, I'm going to tell you what I learned. Life is a lot shorter than you think. You spend so much of it planning, doing, worrying, but what really matters is right in front of you. The people you love. The moments you share. Spend time with your loved ones. Prioritize them. Don't waste time chasing things that won't matter in the end."

Jack and Colleen looked at each other and made an unspoken promise never to go so long without speaking again.

"Be present. Don't get lost in the past. Or caught up in what the future might bring. The only thing you really have is the here and now. And if you don't make it count, well, you'll miss a lot. Actually, you will miss everything."

Mary took this one to heart. She'd been so busy worrying about school and what her future would bring that she often had a hard time simply enjoying the moment. She made a silent promise to her grandfather that she would change all that.

"When I was younger, I took on the role of caregiver from an early age. This followed me into my adulthood, where it prevented me from living life fully. While taking care of others is important, never forget that you matter, too. Don't take on too much. Allow space for personal joy, emotional connection, and balance in relationships."

"I'll never forget when you told me that years ago, Dad," Colleen said.

Thomas smiled at his daughter and then continued. "Remember that, because you matter, ask for help when you need it. It's okay to lean on the people you love. Make your own needs clear. And if someone you are with can't or won't value your needs the way you do, they aren't worth your time."

This one hit Jack hard. He was very much like his father in his younger years and he struggled with asking anyone for assistance. He vowed to humble himself more in the future.

"Learn how to forgive. I spent so many years holding onto grudges, letting anger take root in my heart. But it only makes you bitter. It only eats away at you. It holds you down. It doesn't affect the other person one bit. Let the past go and you will be a happier and healthier person."

Thomas paused to take another sip of water. While he did, Evvie came into the room to check on everyone. "Mr. Thomas, you are awake!" she said excitedly.

"Yes, but this burst of energy isn't lasting long. I don't know if you remember me, but you gave me some sage advice the night my mother died. She was a patient just down the hall. You had just started working here."

"Oh, I remember you, sugar, and your sweet mom. Told me she loved me to the moon and back, how'd ya like that?"

"That definitely sounds like my grandma," Colleen said.

Jack nodded in agreement. "That woman certainly had a lot of round trips to the moon."

Thomas began speaking again. "Life isn't about the big moments; it's about the small ones. Life will pass you by if you spend your time waiting for things to be perfect. Look and find joy in moments that others would find insignificant. The shared laughter, the quiet conversations, impromptu dance parties in the kitchen. Yes, Mary, I remember those."

Mary wiped tears from her eyes and gave her Geepo a gentle hug.

"Remember that doubt comes hand-in-hand with faith, but that faith is something that can get stronger when tested. You will find that your faith can get you through the darkest of times. It is more than just a candle in the darkness, it is a great giant searchlight when you need it most."

Thomas sat down on the bed. He was becoming visibly more tired and all in the room could tell he was losing steam.

"Your grandfather is right about that, sugar," Evvie said, nudging Mary.

"Your loved ones will always be with you, even when they've left this plane. You will think I'm crazy, but I know this for a fact. And I will be looking after you once my journey here is done. Watch for signs."

Evvie nudged Mary again. "I told you, sugar."

Thomas continued on but was starting to take more breaths in between sentences. "None of us was brought into this world to suffer. Life isn't something that is meant to be endured. You should experience as much joy as you can while you are here. Love is a big part of that joy, and I'd argue that it is the true nature of the life that is to come. Experience as much love as you can in the time and offer love to others."

He took a few more breaths, leaned back against the pillows, and continued, "Laugh often every day. You are going to think I'm crazy, but Jesus has a tremendous sense of humor. Why shouldn't He? Humor would have been a powerful tool for Him to create trust, break down barriers, and invite others into the joy of the Kingdom of God."

Mary thought about the last few years of her life and couldn't remember the last time she experienced anything relating to joy. Her area of study was all about helping people going through rough patches in their life. If she didn't inject joy into her life, given her chosen profession, she'd be destined to become someone else's patient. Living with more joy was going to be her number one New Year's resolution.

Thomas felt his eyes get heavy. He knew he'd be drifting back to sleep shortly and realized it was important to get one more message out to his family. His voice was much weaker and they all leaned in to hear, including Evvie.

"I feel as if I have so much more to share with you but I don't have time, so the last thing I will say is to challenge you to find your soul's purpose. You were all born for a reason, something bigger than what you do to earn money. To find your soul's purpose, the first thing you must start doing is living authentically. Don't pretend to be something you aren't. Instead, find the things that bring you joy, that light you up inside. Then you will attract people who add to your light instead of dimming it."

Thomas closed his eyes.

Everyone thought he was finished, but he wasn't. Opening his eyes one last time, he said, "Each of you carries a spark from the Creator. That is what Jesus meant when he said that the Kingdom of Heaven is within you. To find that kingdom, live your calling and bring a joy revolution not only to your lives, but to the rest of the world. These are my wishes for you all. As my mother would say, 'I love you to the moon and back.'"

Joseph closed his eyes.

As he was drifting off, he heard a voice he hadn't heard in over four decades. "Care to take a walk?"

His brother Mick's face came into focus.

# 15

Mary watched her grandfather closely as he drifted back to sleep. At first his breathing was regular, deep, and rhythmic, but it changed on a dime. His breaths became fewer and far between, as if he was waiting to exhale, holding on to each breath knowing another may not come. Then, at the stroke of midnight, a long exhalation was not followed by the sight of his chest rising.

Everyone in the room looked around at each other, unsure of what to do or even how to feel. The shock they felt at the arrival of the moment they'd been anticipating all day prevented both words and tears from coming.

Evvie walked to the bed, placed her fingers on Thomas' carotid pulse and then his wrist and closed her eyes. "I'm so sorry, babies, but Thomas is home now."

Mary looked at her Geepo's body and saw that it already looked different. His coloring had changed dramatically; his pinkish hue was replaced by a yellowish tint. She knew he was no longer in the body he occupied, which was now just an empty shell. She could sense his essence had left, that his soul was beginning its journey home.

The room felt too small, too quiet. Mary sat motionless in the chair beside her grandfather's bed, staring at the space he no longer occupied. A minute ago, he had been there—really there—his voice crackling with the weight of wisdom and time, his eyes full of love and mischief. And now, he was gone.

It had happened so fast. One moment, he was speaking, offering them the last pieces of himself like carefully wrapped gifts.

Colleen let out a quiet sob, one of those fragile, breaking sounds that came from somewhere deep, where words had no meaning. Jack, sitting stiffly beside her, pressed a hand to his forehead like he was trying to hold in something that threatened to spill over.

Mary just sat there, gripping her phone so tightly her fingers ached. It was still recording. She hadn't stopped it. She couldn't. Part of her feared that if she pressed the button, the moment would disappear completely.

A hand touched her shoulder. "You okay, sugar?"

The answer was no, but Mary swallowed against the lump in her throat and nodded.

The silence stretched out, thick and suffocating. There was nothing left to do now. No more water to bring him. No more stories to keep him company. No more whispered reassurances that he wasn't alone. The doing was over, and all that was left was this—this heavy, aching space between what had been and what came next.

Mary hated it.

For months, she had been running on empty, balancing classes, work, and the long, slow decline of the man who had once seemed larger than life. She had spent so much time keeping herself busy, filling every moment with action, because if she stopped—if she really let herself feel—she might fall apart completely.

And yet, his final words had been about exactly that.

"Be present."

"Don't get lost in the past or caught up in the future."

"Take care of yourself, too."

The words rattled around inside her, knocking against the walls she had built to keep herself moving forward. He had known. Of course, he had known. He had seen the same tendencies in himself. The same inability to let go. The same exhaustion that came from carrying too much, from giving and giving until there was nothing left.

Mary looked at him now, peaceful in a way he hadn't been in years. His face was soft, free of pain, of worry. There was nothing unfinished in his expression. No fear. No regret.

She exhaled slowly, forcing herself to unclench her hands. Her whole life, she had been so focused on what came next—school, work, responsibilities, expectations. But right now, sitting in the quiet of this room, she had the strangest feeling that her grandfather was still here. Not in his body. Not in the way she wanted. But in some way that felt just as real.

Evvie nudged her gently. "You know, sugar, he meant every word of what he said. They don't ever really leave us. You just gotta watch for the signs."

Mary wanted to believe that. God, she wanted to believe that. But she didn't know how.

Outside the window, the snowfall had slowed, the thick clouds breaking just enough for a sliver of moonlight to shine through. It landed right on her grandfather's face, illuminating the lines and stories etched into his skin.

Mary blinked hard against the sting in her eyes. Maybe the key to spotting signs was just paying attention.

She reached out, resting her hand lightly over his. It was still warm. She could almost pretend he was still there. But she didn't. Instead, she squeezed once, like she had a thousand times before, and whispered the words he had said to her every night when she was little. "I love you to the moon and back, Geepo."

And for the first time in a long time, she let herself just be.

# 16

Thomas felt an impossible lightness as he drifted free from his body, a sensation so foreign yet so natural that he barely had time to question it. He hovered toward the ceiling, looking down at the scene below—his family, his flesh, the life he had just left behind. It was strange, seeing himself from this vantage point.

Colleen and Jack held his hands tightly, as if sheer will could tether him back to them. Mary sat by his feet, rubbing them gently the way she had in his final days, a silent comfort. Evvie leaned over him, fingers pressed lightly against his carotid artery. After a moment, she turned to the family and shook her head.

"I'm so sorry, babies, but Thomas is home now." she said, her voice soft but certain.

Thomas watched it all unfold with an eerie sense of detachment. Shouldn't he feel something? Regret? Sorrow? The unbearable pull of loss?

But there was none of that. Only peace.

"Why don't I feel anything?" he asked, and as soon as the question left him, he realized he hadn't spoken aloud. He had simply thought it.

Beside him, Mick grinned. His brother looked young again,

the way he had before the illness took him. Before the world had worn him down. His eyes, the same blue daggers Thomas had known all his life, now radiated something more —something deeper.

"The time for pain is over," Mick replied. "From here on out, you will feel nothing but love."

And then it happened.

A warmth unlike anything Thomas had ever known swept over him, wrapping around him like a cocoon. It wasn't just warmth—it was presence. It filled every space inside him, reaching places he hadn't even known were cold. It wasn't like earthly warmth, the kind that fades as soon as the sun sets. This was permanent, infinite, alive.

"Wow," was all he could manage.

Mick chuckled. "You ain't seen nothing yet. Come on, follow me. There are some people waiting for you."

Thomas barely had time to process what was happening before he and Mick began moving—not walking, not flying, but simply existing forward—out of the room, past the bed where his body lay, past the quiet sobs of his family, through the walls that no longer meant anything to him.

The hospital hallway stretched before them, but it was different now. Time and space felt irrelevant. He moved effortlessly, guided by something unseen, yet familiar.

They reached the waiting room. But it was no longer the place where he had been hours earlier that day, sipping bad coffee and dreading the inevitable. It was full—not just with people, but with souls.

A great crowd of familiar faces greeted him, each one more vibrant than he had ever seen them in life. His mother and father stood side by side, looking exactly as they had in his happiest memories. His brother Pete and sister Tina were there too, laughing, radiant with a light he could almost feel. Uncles, aunts, cousins—so many people who had touched his life, now waiting for him with open arms.

And then, the rush of fur.

Thomas let out a joyous laugh as his old dogs bounded toward him—Spanky, Tyler, Murphy and Reilly—all of them, tails wagging, eyes bright, whole again. He dropped to his knees, if knees even existed here, running his hands through their fur, feeling the warmth of their welcome.

"There are dogs in heaven!" Thomas proclaimed with a wide grin.

"Of course there are," said a voice coming from the door that had been locked to Thomas earlier. It was Him. Manny.

But not Manny the nurse. Not the man in scrubs who had spoken in riddles and parables. Now, he stood before Thomas in flowing robes, the kind Thomas had seen a thousand times in sacred art. But the light that surrounded him, the presence that radiated from him, was beyond anything Thomas could comprehend.

Manny smiled. "I told you we'd meet again."

Thomas swallowed hard, glancing at the door. It looked the same as it had before. But now, something deep inside him knew—this time, it would open.

"This door was locked to you earlier," Manny continued, "but now you will find it open. On the other side is the most beautiful place you have ever seen." His eyes softened. "The door is yours to open."

Thomas hesitated. Not out of fear, but out of awe.

His whole life, he had wondered what came next. He had imagined heaven in a thousand different ways, picturing golden gates, endless light, the sound of angelic choirs. But none of those visions had ever come close to this.

He reached for the door, pressing his palm against it, and gently pushed.

The moment the door opened, a light so pure, so vast, so alive spilled into the waiting room. It wasn't blinding—it was embracing. It wrapped itself around him, pulled him forward, filled every empty space he had ever known.

He turned back to Manny one last time. "Am I worthy of this place?"

Manny stepped beside him and placed a hand on his shoulder.

"My child, you were born to be here."

Thomas felt something break free inside him, something he hadn't realized he had been holding onto. Every doubt, every fear, every regret dissolved in that light, leaving only love.

"Come," Manny said, his voice gentle but firm. "Follow me, and let's spend eternity together."

Thomas turned, stepping through the doorway, leaving behind the waiting room—and the world—for the very last time.

# 17

Mary fidgeted in the front row pew as her grandfather's funeral was coming to an end. The air in the church smelled of incense, and Mary busied herself by rereading her grandfather's eulogy as the Communion line dwindled. She wondered how many non-Catholics didn't pay attention to Father Nick's instructions and accidentally made their first, and probably last, Holy Communion that day.

The cantor was finishing the last verse of Bread of Life, while the priest dutifully cleaned his Chalice and placed the remaining consecrated hosts in the tabernacle. Once the congregation moved from kneeling to sitting, he invited Mary up to the lectern to share her words of remembrance.

After placing her printed copy in front of her, Mary looked all around the church and saw many familiar faces. She glanced at the small table placed directly in front of the altar with her grandfather's urn. It was so him, a simple wooden urn, which she thought impossibly too small to contain the greatest man she ever knew.

"Before I begin my words of remembrance, I want to welcome you all and thank Daniel, our cantor, and Alma, our organist, for the beautiful music. I also extend my gratitude to Father Nick for this beautiful Mass. Lastly, I sincerely appreciate the Thomas M. Gallagher Funeral Home in Stamford for making this a special send-off for my grandfather. I also want to thank Geepo for planning all of this down to the music we heard today. Doing so took a lot of pressure off my family during the holidays. Mom always joked that her father was so organized that he likely planned his own funeral. Turns out, Mom, you were right!"

Gentle laughter rippled through the church.

Mary glanced down at her grandfather's urn, took a deep breath and continued. "One thing you may not know about the man we are here to celebrate today is that he taught me how to tie my shoes. It was the day before kindergarten was to begin and he asked me if I knew how to tie my shoes, and I shook my head no. My parents never taught me. He made it his mission that day to teach me, and he did. I'd tell you I thought about him when I was tying my shoes this morning, but I'm wearing heels today."

Another rumbling of laughter swept through the congregation, and Mary became more comfortable in front of the microphone.

"His life lessons for me didn't end with how to tie my sneakers. He taught me the importance of being honest with other people but more importantly with myself. He encouraged me to be my authentic self, to expect in others what they expect in me, and to ask for help when I need it. He taught me the importance of finding joy in the small things and I have a quick story on that."

Mary paused and took a deep breath; she knew this story might evoke some tears.

"After his diagnosis, he knew he didn't have much time. I lived with him at the house up in Fairfield and this past summer he wanted to create a garden in the backyard to attract hummingbirds. So we planted nectar-rich flowers, including trumpet vine, bee balm, and columbine. We looked for native plants with red and orange flowers because these are attractive to hummingbirds, and we hung feeders with water and sugar nearby. He'd spend hours on end just sitting in the backyard waiting for them to come and when one did, he'd get so excited you'd think he'd won the lottery."

Mary gave herself a minute to suppress the urge to cry and then continued. "Well, if you ask me, I was the one who won the lottery when I was born because my Geepo showed me nothing but love. He went to every game I played and every dance and theatre performance I had, even if I was just in the chorus, which is kind of funny since I can't hold a tune."

This earned big laughs from the congregation, some of whom were careful not to laugh too loudly in a church, thinking it might be disrespectful. Mary knew differently, joy is at the very heart of Christ's message.

Mary waited for the laughter to settle down before continuing. "He taught me to show up for the moments that matter in life. His example is one of love and kindness and I will hold all the lessons he taught me in my heart for as long as I live."

Mary paused as a murmur of 'ahhhs' went through the congregation.

"I'm under strict instructions from Geepo to keep this brief, so I will be wrapping it up now. Just a few closing thoughts. First, today is Saturday morning and Geepo would want you to know that this Mass doesn't count toward your Sunday obligation, so if you are Catholic, this parish has a vigil Mass at five o'clock tonight and three Masses tomorrow morning at eight, ten, and eleven-thirty."

This earned a big laugh from the congregation and an even bigger one from Fr. Nick.

"Second, internment will be private and not immediately following this Mass. You are all invited to come back to the family house in Fairfield for an afternoon of food, family, and fun in Geepo's memory. The address is printed on the back of the program. Thank you all."

It is not customary to receive a standing ovation after giving a eulogy, but Mary earned one from the congregation that day. Once everyone settled down, Fr. Nick said a final blessing over Thomas's urn and Mass ended with a lovely rendition of "*May Holy Angels Lead You*."

After greeting attendees with her family in a receiving line after the Funeral, Mary walked to her car alone. Her mother was catching a ride with Uncle Jack, and she was looking forward to a quiet twenty-five-minute ride back to Fairfield from Stamford by herself. After starting the car, Mary was shocked to hear a traditional Marian hymn coming out of her speakers.

> *Bring flow'rs of the fairest,*
> *Bring flow'rs of the rarest,*
> *From garden and woodland*
> *And hillside and vale*
> *Our full hearts are swelling,*
> *Our Glad voices telling*
> *The praise of the loveliest*
> *Rose of the vale.*

Looking at her radio, she saw that it was tuned to The Catholic Channel on satellite radio, which Mary didn't know existed. She had been listening to a podcast on grief on her way down to the church. Then she remembered what Evvie said, be on the lookout for signs.

Turning the volume up, she said. "Well played, Geepo, well played."

**THE END**

## Acknowledgements

This book would not exist without the generous support, wisdom, and encouragement of many people to whom I owe a deep debt of gratitude.

To my editor, Barbra Ellis—thank you for your sharp insight, thoughtful guidance, and steady collaboration. Your direction helped shape this story into something far richer than I imagined. To my agent, Jan Kardys, thank you for your belief in this project and for your steadfast representation.

To Lisa Labozzo, whose unique blend of encouragement and spiritual intuition planted the seed that became this book —thank you for helping me listen to the voice inside that was ready to speak.

To the medical professionals at Sloan Kettering in New York and Holy Cross Hospital in Fort Lauderdale—thank you for the compassion and care you provided my brother and mother in their final months. Your work gave our family precious time and dignity in the face of tremendous loss.

To my father, who endured the unimaginable loss of both his son and his spouse, and to my siblings, who walked with me through the grief of losing a brother and a mother—I see you, I love you, and I am grateful to be on this journey with you.

To my family, who lived with a writer deep in grief and gave me the space to process it the only way I knew how—by putting words on a page. Thank you for your patience, your love, and your grace. Specifically, thank you Nicole for forcing me out of the house when all I wanted to do was stay in bed.

To Carolyn, my sister-in-law, who read an early version of this story, I appreciate your kind words, feedback, and strength in reading this story. I know parts of it may have been difficult to read, but I hope you got a few smiles as well. I miss him too.

And finally, to Fr. David Roman, thank you for your spiritual guidance and for helping me see God's hand even in sorrow. Your presence reminded me that grief and grace often walk hand in hand.

This story was born from pain, but shaped by love. Thank you all for helping me tell it.

— Michael Carlon

Made in the USA
Middletown, DE
09 June 2025

76735275R00074